THROUGH MY FATHER'S EYES

FOR YEARS, MAYER FISCHER SAT WITH HIS SON AND TOLD HIM STORIES OF THE HOLOCAUST SO THE WORLD WOULD NOT FORGET

BARRY FISCHER

DEDICATION

My parents always asked of me two things, that I would promise to share with the World what happened to them, and in doing so, work to make sure the Holocaust never happens again. This book is dedicated to that purpose and to my two ever-loving parents, Mayer, and Blima Fischer from Krakow Poland, to my grandfather, Baruch Fischer, and my great grandfather Aaron Fischer

Table of Contents

FOREWORD

It has been the greatest honor of my life to write a book about my father, Mayer Fischer. The journey of having Mayer Fischer as my father, and Blima Fischer as my mother two Holocaust survivors has served as a profound and constant realization that my life was blessed with parents who were both very special and very different. My sister Anna and I share a unique bond with one another. Because of the tremendous love we received from our parents, we became who we are today.

My father would always tell us, "I lived a good life and I have lost so many family members and friends that I loved. I loved my grandparents, my parents, my aunts, my uncles, and my cousins, and no matter what happened, I never lost my pride. I was always fair with everyone, and no one can ever say that I ever took anything away from anyone."

Then my father would say something truly profound: "What kept me alive in the Holocaust was simple. I always believed that it was my last day, so I might as well take a risk, and this is how I survived."

I still get chills when I recall the story of his father Baruch's death in 1945 in the Melk Concentration Camp, when the German "doctor" chose to administer an injection of gasoline instead of medicine for his wounded leg, and the image of how my father carried his father's dead body to the crematorium will always haunt me.

Then the Nazi SS officer gave my father a big pot of soup as a reward for his voluntarily act of carrying the dead body of another prisoner up to the crematorium. Of course, the officer would never know that the body my father carried was that of his own father.

My father and his brother Nathan shared that incredible celebratory soup in the hell that was the Melk Concentration Camp, and they felt happiness and relief that their father, Baruch, was truly released from that hell. My father's stories showed such cleverness and courage: stories of how he smuggled food into the Krakow Ghetto and then paid off the guards in order to get through the gate with this smuggled wagon of food.

And then there was the terrible day in the City of Krakow when my father's deportation to Treblinka appeared inevitable. By sheer circumstance his brother-in-law, Lanak, would appear out of the chaos at the train station's deportation area, and manage to convince the Nazi SS officer to send my father to the queue of Jews headed to the right ... those assigned to work detail, rather than the to the left, which would have taken my father directly to the gas chamber.

My father shared stories of the daily random selections that occurred in the Krakow Ghetto and at the Plaszow Concentration Camp, the Mauthausen Concentration Camp, the Melk Concentration Camp, and then finally at Ebensee, where my father Mayer and his brother Nathan were liberated by the Allies in 1945.

Over the years, as my father shared the stories of his life, I always yearned to know more. This book honors my father and my mother. With it, I pass on their epic story of courage, human triumph, and dark horror, as well as their enduring wish that the Holocaust and its evil never happens again!

ACKNOWLEDGMENTS

I extend special thanks to the following people who assisted me in the creation of this book. My loving father Mayer Fischer who encouraged me, inspired me, and insisted that this book was of critical importance to make sure the world never forgets! Thank you to Felice Austin, for helping with the interview and initial structure of this book. To Jeffrey Steindorf, my dear friend, thank you for your meticulous editing work. To Jody Isaak, I thank you for assisting me in compiling, titling, editing, and polishing of the text, as well as integrating the photographs into the text. Thanks also to Anne Staples, the court reporter who graciously transcribed Mayer and Blima Fischer's Shoah interviews, which greatly facilitated the process of writing this book. And a big thank you to the greatest love in my life God for his continuous support and guidance. I also would like to thank the United States Holocaust Museum for releasing the 1940s-era photo- graphs for publication.

I extend my eternal gratitude to my father for sharing all of his stories with me since I was a four-year-old boy. I would sit on his knee and he would tell me all of his tales.

Mayer Fischer in 1947

My father wrote this before he died.

In Hebrew, the name Mayer means "giving light." In German it means "leader." Mayer was a firstborn son, a leader, a light bringer, and a fighter.

My name is Mayer Fischer. I am a Holocaust survivor. I fought for family, for friends, for strangers, and for my own life. I learned the double edge of the miracle of survival. By surviving, I led and gave light to life.

My son Bennett wrote this about his grandfather.

My grandfather, Mayer Fischer, was synonymous with courage and strength beyond belief, both internally and externally, from his struggles with his early life in the war to the struggles of relocating to America, to beginning a beautiful family and building a business from the ground up.

I was adopted and I thank all of you for welcoming me so warmly and accepting me, even when at times I felt out of place. Pappy was always going the extra mile to make me feel accepted as a member of this amazing family and most importantly I felt loved.

I want to honor him because when I compare my struggles to what my grandfather went through I have him as a reference and I put myself in his shoes.

Each time I look at the glass half empty and compare whatever I was or am going through, to what he went through for over 94 long years, I am able to find the strength to push on every time.

I love you Pappy, and no words can never convey the level of gratitude I have for you as a person, a role model, and the patriarch of our family. Thank you for being in my life.

ONE

EARLY MEMORIES

When I look at pictures of Poland, they are in black and white, but my memories are in full, vivid color. Krakow, Poland, was a large city. The downtown area resembled New York, filled with big buildings, churches, and apartment complexes. When I was a small child, the buildings looked gigantic. Luckily they were painted so you could tell one from the next.

Krakow's streets were colorful with reds and yellows, browns, and greens. In the summertime, all of the restaurants had outdoor seating. Yellow, purple, and orange flowers bloomed in the street planters, on balconies, and in the markets. The market square filled with farmers selling vegetables, fruits, and grains. As a teenager, I worked at the mill that ground the wheat and corn into grain, which was sold at the markets.

Outside the market square, the city sprawled along the river Vistula. The hills reflected hues of green, and the sky in the late summer was grand and blue.

Wawel Castle, Krakow, Poland, 2012

Krakow in the 1940s

Interior of Krakow's Old Synagogue during the 1940s

The trolley ran until 9 p.m., but many people rode bicycles. There were few cars in the late 1920s. My father owned a bicycle and used it to travel door to door selling Singer sewing machines to countryside farmers' wives.

In the center of Krakow, the large cathedral could be seen from great distances, and one could hear the church bells ringing every hour.

Krakow is an old city founded before the end of the first millennium. Krakow is located in southern Poland, but for several hundred years, during periods known as Partitions, the Prussians, Russians, and Austrian troops controlled this land. During this time Poland ceased to exist or even to appear on maps of Europe. Then when the Polish diaspora communities congregated in 1918, they reestablished the Polish state and Krakow came back to life.

The first Jews resided in Krakow during the early thirteenth century. By 1931, more than 55,000 Krakow residents identified themselves as Jews in the Polish census. This constituted close to one-fourth of the total population.

Aaron Fischer, a learned man, Mayer Fischer's grandfather

My grandfather, Aaron Fischer, was a great man. People regarded him as a saint. A man of wisdom. When an impoverished Jew would die, Aaron washed and buried them. He was religious and a student of the great books the Torah, Talmud, and Chamush. They called him *Tzadikim*, which means "doing all good things for God for free."

Aaron and my grandmother, Blindel, had four children. My father Baruch Fischer was their second child, and then came his brother, Leiblich, and two sisters, Hayka and Rachel. My mother's name was Rose Felcher.

My parents met sometime in the early part of 1917. They were both looking for work. As a widow with a young daughter named Lydia, my mother was in great need of work at that time.

My parents had a short courtship, as most people did in those days, and married in Krakow in 1918. As newlyweds, they lived in Lishke and ran a housewares store. Then the war came. And it was a war unlike any other.

My father went to fight in the Austrian Army. My mother learned she was expecting me after he left for the war. When I was born, he took leave from the army and was thrilled to see me, his firstborn male child. I recall a picture, which has since been lost, in which my father was wearing his army uniform adorned with a bright sash across his chest. He looked very young holding me, his newborn son. When the war ended, he came home for good. That was in 1920.

My memories of my father are of Saturdays at shul (synagogue) in Lishke. He was a religious man and encouraged the same of his family. We went to shul together every Saturday. He covered his head and mouthed the words of the prayers he sang. I remember his great singing voice.

On other days of the week he worked at the hardware store or would go out on his bicycle to sell sewing machines. As a child I remember him rising early in the morning, bags loaded with advertisements and brochures, setting out on his bicycle, then returning in the evening with signed contracts that were fulfilled by the Singer Sewing Machine Company. My mother helped in the store and cooked.

I often spent weekday evenings reading in my room after supper. I recall hearing my mother singing in the kitchen, her melodically happy voice filling our house as she worked. She was always singing. She had so much to do with the kids, the store, and the housework, and yet she was always singing.

As she tucked in my shirt and straightened my collar each day, she would smooth out my hair and ask, "Mayer, have you done your schoolwork for the day?"

"Yes, Mama."

"Nathan?" She held out her hand as Nathan took his turn to approach her. He reluctantly stepped forward because he hated when she used her thumb to rub the dirt off his cheeks. He had a tendency to get into everything, even very early in the morning.

"Boys, be good, stay together, and behave. Now go learn." She would always say this as she gently pushed us out the door. As we walked down the steps, we could hear her melodic humming behind us.

Nathan and Mayer Fischer in 1948

We all helped our mother around the house because she had so much to do. There was the busy store and four children to attend to. Lydia was seven years older than me and a big help at home. Later when I was twelve, we hired a girl who would come in to do the wash, get water from the well, wash the floor, and do other things around the house.

I am sure that no one else had a dog like ours. We named him Wolf, because he was big, white, and looked just like one. He was a wonderful playmate, a faithful watchdog, and he guarded the house better than any police officer could. A good-natured dog, Wolf was never on a leash because he didn't need one. He was loyal and happy. He liked to make the rounds and to protect the apartment. Often, when Nathan and I came home from school, Wolf would be there waiting. He would let us scratch behind his ears while he kept his eyes on the road behind us, and smiling the way dogs do. The other kids in the neighborhood loved our dog. Really, I think they were just jealous!

Wolf was not allowed in the house. He stayed in his doghouse outside. When there was any suspicious activity he would bark loudly and mean enough to scare away any trouble faster than law enforcement ever could!

Late one night before the real trouble in Krakow started, we were all home in bed, asleep. Wolf started barking his loud, deep bark just outside the door. We could sense that something was very wrong. My father got up to check. He ran down the stairs on the side of the store. He then slowly opened the door and peered out onto the street. Wolf continued growling but my father saw nothing, and whatever or whomever had been there was gone. Up and down the quiet street all the neighbors were sleeping. It felt eerie. Wolf quieted down and everyone went back to bed, but I couldn't help but feel something sinister was out there in the darkness quietly waiting and scheming.

Mayer Fischer, age 10

School Days

The Catholic priest came to town every Thursday. He told his students that the Jews killed Jesus. That was the whole story. They programmed the kids to hate the Jews to hate *us*.

We were the only Jews in our public school, except for a boy named Josef, but his mother picked him up every day, so he avoided the after school bullying. They came for Nathan after school, waylaying him behind the utility shed by the oak trees. "Jew!" they taunted. "Jesus killer!" Nathan was scrawny. There were four or five of them, and he already saw that he could not win. He put his books down, outside of the pack of kids who punched, pushed, and shoved him. I would run to join him. We stood back to back, fearless in our fighting stances. They outnumbered us. But for every punch they got in, we gave back at least two or three!

When the bullies heard the janitor banging around in the shed, they looked up suddenly and took off running some swaggering, and some staggering away! We held our position until they were out of sight. I recall that the ground was strewn with a mix of oak leaves and Nathan's school papers. When he bent down to pick them up, the blood from his hands the knuckles bloody from the hard licks he'd gotten in smeared the white paper. He took a deep breath. My brother Nathan was five years younger than me, and still a baby in many ways.

"Come on," I told Nathan. "We gave them two black eyes for every one we got! Let's go home."

Nathan said nothing. I could see the frustration on his face as he wiped his nose on his sleeve and took a deep breath. He looked up at me as we walked home. I was his big brother. I knew he was proud of me because I always came to his rescue. The truth was that we both had one another to watch our backs. Looking out for each other became our lifelong story. It is how we survived the war and thrived afterwards for the rest of our lives. My brother Nathan and I worked together in business after the war until the time of our retirement in 1984.

As a child I always looked forward to Fridays and holidays. Every holiday was my favorite. I liked holidays because my father was home. Rosh Hashanah, Yom Kippur, Sukkot, Passover, and Chanukah: These were all memorable celebrations in our home and in our community. Every Friday evening and Saturday, I observed the Sabbath by attending shul with my father and my brother Nathan.

Friday nights were special and beautiful moments in our family life. There was great excitement every Friday as my mother, aided by my sisters, Hella and Lydia, prepared the food and the table for Shabbat. My father, Nathan, and I went to shul to pray. After Shabbat services we returned home. My mother always lit the special candles to welcome the Sabbath into our home. I will always remember the image of my mother covering her eyes with a lily doily while praying the blessing over the candles, welcoming the Shabbat into our home. The food we ate on Friday night was always special: gefilte fish, chicken, turkey, potatoes, vegetables, and chicken soup. We said the blessing over the challah bread and then the wine.

On Saturday, the whole family attended shul. It was magnificent! The synagogue was filled with wood benches and separate sides for men and women. A wooden rack adorned with silver displayed prayer scrolls covered with embroidered velvet fabric with the Torah pointers. There were casted bells and crowns on the scroll handles and a breastplate inscribed with beautiful shapes and scenes from the Bible. Everything was in silver, to honor the holy of holiest, our beloved Torah.

The place where they held the Torah, the Arc, was covered with stunning wooden doors, engraved with the Ten Commandments. Each of the two Torahs was beautifully handcrafted, the words handwritten by a holy man and his scribe. Each took more than one year to write. Traditionally, the scribe would sit in the light to keep his mind clear and stay connected to God. After each time he said God's name (which was often in the Torah) he would have to bathe himself in a *mikva*, a bath in which Jewish ritual purifications are performed.

Each Torah was kept on two wooden rollers, the pages glued, side by side, to form a single sheet from beginning to end. It was rolled open during services, placed on the altar, and read with a silver pointer to help the reader (chasan) while he was praying during services. When the rabbi, cantor, or chasan completed his Torah reading, it was rolled up and tied with a soft cloth to protect the parchment. The two rollers were rolled together and bound with a satin band that held them together, and then covered with a beautiful velvet cover that was embroidered with silver and gold, with Hebrew words of blessing from God.

My best memories of my father are of him standing or sitting in the shul, praying, reading Hebrew, singing and adoring God. Despite the mounting discrimination against the Jews in Poland, life was amazingly hopeful.

When I was five years old, my father taught me the Hebrew letters in the *siddur* (prayer book) so I could read along with him. My father sat with me at the dining room table and, step by step, patiently taught me how to read and write the twenty-two Hebrew letters. Once I learned the Hebrew letters, my father taught me how to read the Hebrew prayers. He then explained every word in Hebrew so I could understand its meaning. He was passing down the Jewish wisdom that every Jewish father passed down from generation to generation: Jewish law, tradition, and the ability to pray.

Torah scroll from the early 1900s.

Torah ornaments from the 1800s and 1900s

Chanukah Menorah from the 1930s

Chanukah Menorah from the 1930s

Friday night Sabbath Table from the 1930s

I loved going to shul and praying with my father and being next to him every Saturday and on all Jewish holidays. We enjoyed the walk to shul, which was only a few doors down from our home. We were observant, Orthodox Jews living in Krakow.

There were about 500 people that attended our shul. We were a strong community of families that met every week and, on all holidays, to share our experience in prayer.

My father was often honored, called up to Torah. He would take me along, and I stood next to him proudly as he said the *Barucha.*

"Baruch ata Adonai ham vorach lolam va-ed."

"Baruch ata Adonai ham vorach lolam va-ed."

I was so proud and honored. After the reading, every person in the shul would shake my father's hand and receive "the light" from the Torah. The light was passed on to the entire congregation in this manner. The honor of standing closest to the Torah as we were reading and singing was the highest honor that was bestowed upon a family.

Summers

Every summer my big sister Lydia and I would go to our grand parents' home. How I loved going to visit them! It was different from being in Krakow. They lived thirty kilometers outside of the city. The ride there was pleasant and scenic, winding along the Vistula River until both buildings and people appeared less and less. The dominant color of this rustic paradise was green. I will remember those summer weeks with moments of carefree fun alternating with religious contemplation forever. My father's parents, Aaron and Blindel, were even more religious than my father. During our visits we read the Torah every day and did many religious things. I credit much of my personal and religious identity to these visits.

My grandparents also worked very hard. Arising before the sun each day, they would arrive by 6:00 a.m. at the local *ayarmak*, which was a type of outdoor bazaar or flea market. I would go with them when I was visiting. Every week they would travel to a different marketplace. Colorful ribbons, lace, scarves, and other beautiful things that they made were loaded into their wagon. They wrapped them carefully, like presents, and kept them safe upon the wagon until we got to our destination. The markets were each 6 to 10 kilometers away.

I liked to help my grandparents. I especially enjoyed watching the ladies who came to shop for their niceties. I remember how they would hold up the different colors, run their fingers along the satin and lace as if the touch of it would tell them something. There were so many pretty girls with their mothers! Sometimes they smiled at me during these exchanges which equally thrilled and embarrassed me and I would wonder what they would make with these ribbons and lace.

My grandparents taught me how to be a good salesman and how to run a business. The one thing that was always stressed was the concept of "quality."

The Circus

Even with all the work, study, and religious celebrations, I still had time to just be a kid. I have vivid memories of when the circus came to town so strong that I can still smell the wet sawdust and the delicious popcorn. The circus would roll in around sunset, and along with it was a caravan of dilapidated old trucks, which transported the exotic animals. A flashy old convertible of English-make led a big van painted orange, blue, and green. I imagined the man inside was blond and had a handlebar mustache, but I couldn't see much in the gathering dark.

By morning, the whole circus was set up. Red and white tents with three central stakes appeared like magic. It was bigger than I had imagined. The smell of animals and hay was pungent. Now, I had never actually seen an elephant but I knew that all of the tremendous piles of poop on the ground in front of me had to be made by one!

When we entered the tent, the air was thick and dark. My eyes adjusted slowly to this inner world, which seemed to me to be from another planet. I wondered about the kind of people that lived in the circus. There were people with paint on their bodies, people in bright clothing, and women wearing feathers and wings. Bleachers were set up for the patrons to sit in. Everyone took his or her seat as a man with a black face and wearing nothing but a scanty leopard skin climbed up a rope. I was fascinated because I had never seen a black man before. I had heard that they existed, but had never seen one in Poland.

It was hard to focus on all of the events and sensations! The smell of popcorn, ladies jumping from rope to rope, twirling batons; clowns crying and then falling down. And in the center of it all was the jaunty ringmaster, an amazing man in a top hat and sporting a handlebar mustache, just exactly as I imagined.

I was disappointed that I still saw no elephant when finally, in the corner of my eye, I saw fire erupt! To my astonishment, a man was jumping through a flaming hoop. It was magnificent! The awesome sight more than made up for the absence of a pachyderm.

Lydia was seven years older than me and had already gone to college. She was a teacher at a Catholic school. It was rare at that time for a Jewish woman to go to college. She went to Yaganasko University in Krakow, and was the only Jew to finish. It was even more rare for a Jewish woman to be a teacher. But Lydia was smart. She was always teaching me and helping me with my homework, and she even found the time to tutor other children. I loved to have her around. While she wasn't pretty in the traditional way, people felt her wise and recognized her beautiful spirit and wanted to get to know her. Nothing ever held her back, not even the limp caused by a birth defect of her hip. She married late but well. Her husband's name was Lanak

Bolva, and he dearly loved her. As a lawyer he was very helpful to our family when our childhood days became a distant memory, and the war changed our world forever.

Now, what we didn't know in 1938 was that the Germans had already positioned spies in Poland. They knew everything and had lists of all the Jewish families living in Krakow. They even had my name and my entire family's names recorded. They even knew who we were and where we lived. The Germans had all of these records before the war. They were so prepared.

I later learned that they even had a record of what I did every day and where I worked! The records continued throughout the war. I know this because the German government sent me these records after the war. And it was this information that forced them to approve my pension. I am ninety-four years old and the German government still sends me a pension for all of the work I did in the concentration slave camps during the war.

Entrance to Plaszow Concentration Camp. The sign reads "Albeit Macht Frei." *In English: "Work makes you free"*

TWO

INVASION– SEPTEMBER 1939

I joined the Polish Army when I turned eighteen. They gave me a uniform, a pair of shoes, and a horse. Historically, Poland was known for its cavalry. But in 1939, when the Germans invaded, it became a test of strength between their military tanks and our finest Polish warhorses.

I even remember a patriotic band was playing somewhere as a show of support for our army, which became the soundtrack to a pitiful scene. Very young men and very good horses marched to their deaths against Germany's monstrous metal war machines. We had a few cannons which we fired, but it was a pathetic attempt. I distinctly recall the mingled stench of sweat, blood, gasoline, and freshly opened earth, as we watched with horror as the tanks gashed huge tire tracks in the ground, mowing down flowerbeds and gardens. Wild fear shone in the eyes of the horses as our riders tried to control them. The sound of hooves against the road was barely audible against the thunder of the German invasion. Then, the band went silent and we surrendered. Or so I heard. Three columns rode into battle against the tanks, and they were all dead. The rest of us were held back. And thus I survived.

A German commander lined up all the young men that were left and asked who could speak German. I raised my hand. He said to me: "All of your cavalry that rode into battle has been killed. We are not going to kill the remaining soldiers that are here. My advice to you, and to everyone here: As long as you work for the Germans you will survive."

Then he asked, "Who amongst you are Jews?" We had seven Jews in our army unit, but no one moved. Then he sent us all home.

Within seven days the war was over for us. We surrendered our remaining cavalry and cannons. Though I never received any actual experience fighting the Germans during my seven days in the army, I was about to bravely fight for my life, and for the lives of my family members.

Krakow had been invaded. It was the first major city to have been invaded, and the Polish army had surrendered. The German officer's words stayed with me: "You should get a job, work, and even if you are in prison, you will survive."

I know now that the advice from that German officer, from my enemy, would play an integral part in what would keep me alive throughout the war. I always worked, and God made it possible for me, to survive.

It took the Germans just four weeks to take all of Poland. They were heading for Stalingrad, but the Russians had a third column, a hidden army, within the Polish citizenry. I remember that the Russians had all-white uniforms, which camouflaged them in the snow. Their very warm uniforms gave them a huge advantage over the Germans. The Russians were able to defend Stalingrad.

Nathan and I decided to try to run away to Russia. We walked for two weeks toward the Russian border. We went to peoples' homes asking for food, as beggars, for even a small piece of bread. The Polish people were helping because it was wartime. I was eighteen and Nathan was only thirteen. We hiked to the

Russian border and considered joining the Russian Army. There, we saw that the Germans were advancing on Warsaw. I thought that perhaps Poland could defend itself, but the Polish army quickly collapsed. Nathan and I were able to make a telephone call to our father, and we discussed what we had seen.

"Look," our father finally said, "you better come home. Whatever happens, at least we will be together." My brother and I agreed.

When Nathan and I returned home to Krakow, we learned from Germans occupying the city that there was an enamel factory run by a man named Oskar Schindler. My father, brother, and I worked in Schindler's enamel factory.

Entrance to Oskar Schindler's enamel factory in Krakow, 1940

Oskar Schindler (left) with a horse and unidentified man

Oskar Schindler (second from left) partying with the Nazis

THREE

RESETTLEMENT

In November 1939, it was announced that all Jews aged twelve years and older had to wear armbands with a yellow Star of David on them. The SS and Wehrmacht troops started blocking off entire streets in order to loot the Jewish homes and shops. The homes of the Jewish community were also confiscated, with the best apartments going to German officers and their families. Many young Jewish men were sent to forced labor camps in the small towns and villages of the Krakow district. In April 1940, Hans Frank, the German lawyer who became Nazi Germany's chief jurist and Governor-General of occupied Poland's General Government territory, announced that Krakow would become the "cleanest" city in the General Government. What he meant was "without Jews."

Hans Frank intended to keep this promise, so on May 18, 1940, the Nazis commenced resettlement orders throughout a large part of the Jewish population in Krakow. According to this order only 15,000 working Jews were permitted to stay in the city with their families. The remaining 15,000 Jews were forced into the Krakow Ghetto. By August 15, 1940, many of the Jews had been resettled from Krakow into towns and villages around the capital. One day my father, Baruch Fischer, was taken by the SS. We thought he was dead, but a day later he returned home. For an entire day and night, he was tortured and beaten. My father was never the same after that.

The Big Removal to the Ghetto

The ghetto was set up not in the historical Jewish quarter of Kazimierz, but rather in Podgorze on the southern bank of the Vistula River. All Jews who lived in Krakow had to move into the ghetto by March 20, 1941. Everywhere people were on the move, carrying their possessions and looking for a place to live. My family and I took up residence in an apartment.

Outside the ghetto, four guarded entrances were created. There was the main gate on Limanowski Street, another gate at Podgorski Market on Limanowski Street (only for army vehicles), a third gate on Lwowska Street, and a fourth gate at Zgoda Square.

The resettlement of Jews into the Krakow Ghetto, May 18, 1940

The resettlement of Jews into the Krakow Ghetto, 1940

The resettlement of Jews into the Krakow Ghetto, 1940

Using a riverboat to resettle Jews into the Krakow Ghetto, 1940

Crossing the bridge into the Krakow Ghetto, 1940

Jews bringing their belongings into the Krakow Ghetto, 1940

Jews being marched into the Krakow Ghetto, 1940

Jews bringing what they could carry into the Krakow Ghetto, 1940

Jews being marched into the Krakow Ghetto, 1940

*Resettlement into the
Krakow Ghetto, 1940*

*Resettlement into the
Krakow Ghetto, 1940*

*Resettlement into the
Krakow Ghetto, 1940*

Jews congregated inside the Krakow Ghetto, 1940s

Ghetto Wall

Most of the houses in the ghetto were old and dilapidated. Before the war 3,000 inhabitants lived in the ghetto area, but now more than 15,000 people were crowded into that same space. According to the regulations, four families had to share a single flat. Alternatively, one apartment window was allocated for every three people. Because of the overcrowded housing, many people spent their time in the streets. In October 1941, around 6,000 Jews from surrounding villages were sent into the ghetto. Hunger became the biggest problem. The daily ration of bread for each person was 100 grams. An additional 200 grams of sugar or fat was provided monthly. The main food was potatoes. Most of the Jews were forced to work in ghetto workshops and factories, mainly as part of the German Wehrmacht (armed forces) or Luftwaffe (air force).

My family and I left our home and joined other families with just a few possessions. We were to live in these cramped living quarters in the ghetto. At first, there was nowhere to go and nothing to do except worry or go crazy. This is when I started to think about God.

I believed in God as a child when my grandparents took me to shul. At thirteen I proudly underwent the *bar mitzvah* ceremony. I loved the Jewish holidays that kept my father home with us. I believed when my mother sang, I heard the rain fall. I believed in God when I fought off the mean-natured schoolboys who said that I killed Jesus. When Germany invaded Poland, I still had faith. I believed when I sang the national anthem, when I said my prayers, and when we listened to the radio. I believed in my father.

However, there came a time when I lost faith during a deeply dark moment in the ghetto. I was on the ninth floor of a building, and I saw several soldiers fighting over some poor Jew's meager possessions. They were laughing, drinking whiskey, and holding up their glasses like New Year's revelers, without a care in the world. I knew that my life meant nothing to them. All of us knew that. I saw one of the soldiers become frustrated about something. The scene was a bit chaotic with women and children milling about, and there was a lot of noise. Suddenly a cherubic little child ran toward his mother. The frustrated soldier grabbed the child by the foot, lifted him up, and threw him out of that ninth floor window.

I witnessed this callous and horrific act and thought, *"Can I believe? Can I believe in anything?"*

After that day, I kept my head down. But at the same time I ceased caring. I took more risks because I didn't care about being caught. I figured that I was probably going to die anyway. This way of thinking made me a survivor.

Identification cards were supplied to many Jews before the first deportation from the ghetto took place. Between May 30 and June 8, 1942, the SS would unilaterally decide the fate of those of us who would stay in the ghetto and those who would be subject to deportation. SS-Hauptsturmführer Wilhelm Kunde, the notorious SS officer, was responsible for these deportations.

On May 31, all persons without a card had to gather on Zgoda Square. Jewish policemen were assigned to round up the people in their houses and bring them to Zgoda Square. During the two first days of this "action," 4,000 Jews were deported. They were told that they were going to the Ukraine to work. Then the columns of deportees were led to the Plaszow Railway Station, where they were stuffed into waiting train cars. As the trains departed the station, those onboard still believed they were headed for workcamps in the Ukraine. It was all a big lie, of course. Those trains with all of those Jews were headed to the Belzec Death Camp.

Building of the wall to close in the Krakow Ghetto, 1940

German officer checking the identification cards of Jews (with yellow Star of David armbands) in the Krakow Ghetto, 1941

German officers checking the identification papers, 1941

German officers checking identification papers, 1941

It was around this time that the German industrialist Oscar Schindler and Scmielski began collecting workers for their factories. If you worked for Schindler, you had some measure of protection. Luckily, I got a job at Schindler's factory, so all I had to do was show my card and leave the ghetto to go to work. I wasn't paid for my work but at least I was fed. The freedom that my work papers provided me gave me the ability to run a little side business trafficking goods and food into the ghetto from the outside. This was invaluable to ghetto occupants because there was never enough food.

I was paid with cigarettes, and because I was not a smoker, the cigarettes were easy currency, and I could trade for food and clothing or whatever my family needed.

I would often sneak out of the ghetto. This was, of course, very dangerous. I had a special work pass and rather than heading to the factory, I would travel to see the farmers outside of the city, where I traded clothes from the ghetto for food. There was one kind farmer's family that gave me bread, and I gave them blankets in return. In order to get in and out of the ghetto, I made a deal with a German guard that I paid a few *slottas* (Polish money) to for passage in and out of the ghetto.

The gates of the Krakow Ghetto, 1940

Ghetto gates

A mother and child in the ghetto, 1941

Another gate of the Krakow Ghetto

Jews being lined up and shot inside the Krakow Ghetto, 1941

Wall that closed in the Krakow Ghetto

Barbed wire enclosure of the ghetto. 1940-41

Jews trying to stay warm inside the ghetto, 1940-41

Waiting on line for food in the ghetto, 1941

Life in the ghetto, 1941

German officers in the ghetto

Life inside the ghetto

In front of the synagogue

Life inside the ghetto, 1941

FOUR

THE KRAKOW GHETTO

When Poland surrendered, everything quickly changed, and those with any Jewish heritage was searched out and forced to wear identifying armbands. One by one, all of our freedoms were stripped away. Eventually my family and I, like the rest of the Jews, were forced by the SS to leave our home and live in the Krakow Ghetto. The ghetto was in another part of town, where multiple families were now crammed into apartment buildings. Incredibly, some fifteen thousand Jews were crammed into a mere 3,167 rooms.

A wall surrounded the ghetto, and the side that faced toward the Aryans had no windows, because all of them had been bricked up. The wall's imposing height and tombstone-like panels not to mention the gate that was guarded around the clock by the SS served to break the spirits of those of us held prisoner within.

According to German sources, 68,482 Jews lived in Krakow and the surrounding villages in November 1939. It was one of the largest Jewish communities in Poland.

I would also bribe the Polish police in exchange for passage in and out of the ghetto. The going rate was 10 or 20 *slottas*, which I paid in full one day prior to my intended trip. The police were reliable because they always needed the money. I was even allowed to bring a horse and wagon to hide as much as thirty pounds of flour under the seat, which I brought to a bakery that had agreed to make bread for us. That entire trip was risky but also necessary for my family's survival. I was always risking my life in this way.

The German police were not usually posted around the ghetto, and they would rarely see me because the same Polish police who were paid to allow my passage out also controlled the entrance and exit. In this way I was able to travel in and out of the ghetto two to three times a week. And on the days that I missed work at the factory, my brother Nathan would register me as present.

During our time in the ghetto, the Germans employed *barrackinbau*, which was the given name to the construction workers hired from the Pilefsky Company for the construction of the barracks. It was here that my brother and I worked as carpenters. Schindler's company, Amalia, made things for homes, as well as munitions for the war. Nathan and I worked alongside our cousins, Yosak and Heshak Felcher, loading the components of the barracks onto a freight train. These pre-built barracks consisted of four pieces for the front, two pieces for the side, and two pieces for the top. The Germans would transport the barracks wherever they needed them. Upon delivery, the barracks were easily assembled with screws and by piecing together the walls, doors, and windows. I remember how heavy those pieces were, but my brother and I were very strong. This was just the beginning of the work that we would do for the Germans during the war.

Christian Polish workers didn't want us to work because they needed those jobs themselves. It was a desperate time for everyone. There were so many people that couldn't find work because Germans didn't have to pay the Jews. We Jews accepted the grim reality that slaves did most of the jobs, and we recognized that we *were* slaves with sweat dripping off of our dirty faces.

There was one time when I remember turning around to see a Polish worker picking up a chisel and pointing it at my cousin Yosak. That angry Pole told my cousin that if he continued to work, then he would kill him. We all stood there frozen for a moment. Then suddenly Yosak reached down and grabbed a hammer! Eyes blazing, he raised it and rushed at that Pole. Then, stopping mere inches from his face, he shouted, "Leave me alone or I'll kill *you* now!" The Pole backed away and no one ever bothered Yosak after that!

Those Polish workers did not always understand that we had no choice but to work or be shipped out to Auschwitz. For instance, the barracks manufacturer, Scmieleski in Krakow, utilized 30 percent Jews from the ghetto and 70 percent Polish workers.

The Poles brought food and traded with us for things we could find or make in the ghetto clothing mostly. We also traded items that were left behind by those who had been deported and sent to the camps.

The ghetto's Polish Odermen accompanied the SS any time a Jew who lived in the ghetto was arrested. These Oderman lived in the ghetto as well but were living in better barracks. Sometimes they would even rob us and when they did, since we were Jews, we could not say a word.

During our time in the Krakow Ghetto, the SS came through periodically to carry out their liquidations, and at those times they would always separate us into two groups. There was the group that was headed to Auschwitz and the group headed to work.

Once, the Germans caught me in a place where I was not supposed to be, and they ordered me into a group that they were sending out by train to Auschwitz. On this particular day, sheer luck brought me into contact with my brother-in-law Lanak, who was the lawyer who carried out the record-keeping for the Germans, so they would know who was going where. Lanak saw me on the platform at the train in front of the barracks in line to be sent to the death camp. I was actually thinking, "This is it, this is the end. Now I am leaving my family."

Then, through the line of people, I saw Lanak, who was rushing over to me. He asked me frantically, "What are you doing here?" I told him that I had been caught where I wasn't supposed to be, so I was being punished.

Lanak quickly took my papers, and I watched him disappear. He changed my papers so that they had the right stamp, indicating that the Germans needed me to stay and work. Then he grabbed me off the side of the platform of Jews going to Auschwitz, and shoved me into the line of Jews along with my brother and father, who were all to be assigned to work detail. On that day Lanak miraculously saved my life!

I later learned that Lanak had somehow arranged for papers to allow him to go to Switzerland and America. To do this he would need to get out of the ghetto. With those papers he planned to go to the American Embassy in Switzerland, and then on to America. But there was a Jewish policeman, Sigil, who hated Lanak. Sigal was jealous of Lanak and always caused problems for him. Another man named Leo Weitzman told Sigal that Lanak had the papers to leave the ghetto, and the word was out. Sigal told Schindler, and the very next day the SS took Lanak to an area called Vayovagoka. There, the SS shot him and took him to the crematorium. Lanak was only twenty-six years old. That beautiful man who had saved my life had lost his own just because he couldn't keep a secret and jealousy of another Jew.

After the war, I looked for Sigil, the Jewish policeman that turned in Lanak. I wanted to have him arrested and have him tried in court. He knew I was looking for him, and he hid. He never came to any meeting where the survivors met after the war. I was told he was seen in Danzig, on the Baltic Sea, in Poland. I was unable to get there and arrest him. If I had, he would have been tried, convicted, and executed because we had three witnesses offering testimony about his crimes. But alas, he got away.

After Lanak was killed, my mother and my sister Hella were shipped out to Auschwitz; tragically, they both died there. My other sister, Lydia, was also condemned, but miraculously she survived the selections in Auschwitz, despite her defective hip and pronounced limp, and lived to the ripe old age of ninety-five. Lydia died in 2007 of complications from Alzheimer's disease in Marin County, California, leaving behind one son, Marvin, who had three children. Marvin became a scuba diver, and he and his wife Beth and two children live on the Island of Granada.

I also recall that we had a Polish girl who worked in our home as a maid and housekeeper for us for many years, so we gave her everything in our home when we left for the ghetto. Our Polish maid promised us that she would bring things into the ghetto for us, and every week, she risked her own life as she smuggled in small care packages to help keep us alive.

At the beginning of every week, at a certain point in the morning, we would meet at the wire. I remember those cold mornings when every- thing looked gray in our once colorful city. My hat pulled down tight around my ears, and my head bowed, I would go to the place where I was to meet her. Because I had a special working card from Schindler, I could walk freely out of the ghetto, and it was always so nice to see her smile. While we talked about the family, she would slip me a small package of butter or cheese. The meetings were necessarily short. She was only able to give me small things because I couldn't hide larger bundles on my person. When things got worse, she became afraid. All of this abruptly ended when we were sent out of the ghetto.

Most of the Krakow Jews lived in the historical Jewish district, known as Kazimierz. Many Jewish families had flourished there since 1867 and had their own businesses throughout the entire city. Even today one can visit old Jewish houses and the synagogue in Kazimierz. It is the only historical Jewish district in a large Polish city that was not destroyed during the war.

On September 6, 1939, Krakow was captured by German troops and the city became the capital of the newly established *Generalgouvernement*, led by *General -gouverneur* Hans Frank. He chose the famous Wawel Castle as his residence. Soon after, the Nazis ordered all synagogues closed and established the *Judenratas*, a Jewish council to act as a liaison between the Germans and the Jewish communities.

German police guarding the ghetto gate

Deportation

Not enough people were selected for deportation to satisfy the SS. Many Jews were simply killed on Zgoda Square or in the streets. On June 4, 1942, 600 people were killed in the ghetto. On the last day of this "action," 7,000 Jews from Miechow, Jedrzejow, and Slomniki (villages near Krakow) were deported, together with Krakow Jews.

After the first deportations, many people in the ghetto discussed the fate of their relatives and comrades. Many Jews were lead to believe that these deportees who arrived in the Ukraine were living in good conditions. But several weeks after the deportations, a certain Pole, whose Jewish wife had also been deported from Krakow, was told by Polish workers that those deportees were at the Belzec Concentration Camp, and the truth spread quickly throughout the ghetto. By the end of June, the ghetto's physical area had been reduced.

Deportation from the ghetto into the concentration camps, 1942

Deportation to the concentration camps, 1942

SS officer overseeing the Jews headed for the Concentration Camps, 1942

Jews headed to the Concentration Camps, 1942

SS officer overseeing Jews ordered to the train station,

headed for the Concentration Camps, 1942

Jews being marched to deportation, 1942

Jews being loaded onto the train, 1942

Jews being guarded at the Krakow Train Station, 1942

Jews being guarded at the train station, 1942

The Second Deportation

On October 28, 1942, the largest and cruelest deportation took place in Krakow. In front of the *Arbeitsamt* (job center), children were taken from their parents. In some cases, entire families were selected. Almost everyone had assumed that those people were "privileged."

But actually those who were sick or were invalids were either killed outright or deported. Children from the orphanage were all shot near the town. The teachers who voluntarily accompanied them were killed as well. Afterwards, there were many suicides. In the course of a few days, 4,500 Jews were deported to Belzec and approximately 600 were killed on the spot. The word was also out that Belzec was the deadly terminus of the deportation trains.

In November 1942, Jews from the ghetto were sent to the SS forced labor camp in Plaszow, a suburb of Krakow. Among them were the Jews who worked in Oskar Schindler's enamel factory. As portrayed in Thomas Keneally's 1982 novel *Schindler's Ark* and in Steven Spielberg's 1993 film *Schindler's List*, Oskar Schindler bravely tried to protect and help his Jewish workers during the liquidation of the ghetto.

Then, in December 1942, the ghetto was divided into two parts: "Ghetto A" for workers and "Ghetto B" for non-workers. Those in Ghetto B were to be deported, as soon as possible.

FIVE

LIQUIDATION OF THE GHETTO

"They were separating us ...

we never saw my mother and sister again."

In a single day, the Germans completely liquidated the ghetto. The SS woke us early, and there they were: an entire battalion headed by the dreaded Commander Göeth, who was sitting on his horse, with Oskar Schindler also on horseback by his side.

We heard the sounds of heavy boots on the landings. I recall that I was in our apartment with my family, and we were all terrified. I heard guns smashing doorknobs and the thunder of doors being kicked open as we were all ordered into the square. Women formed a line on the left; the men did likewise on the right. My father, Nathan, and I stayed together on the right. My mother and Hella went left.

How can one speak about the separation of families? How can you measure the pain that a man feels when his beloved wife, who sang while she worked, along with his youngest daughter, barely eleven, are both savagely taken from him?

On that day, I watched my mother and sister go. No one knew exactly what was happening, but there was a dark, foreboding feeling as the guards marched the women away. Rose and Hella looked frightened as they looked back at us, their eyes wide with terror. No one had a choice. The Germans were so powerful, with their coldly efficient guns and their muscular, well-trained viscous police dogs. Many Jews were killed on the spot. Shot in the streets. The Germans claimed that the Jews were trying to run away. Some ran to the fence. They were electrocuted on the electrical wire that encircled the ghetto like a noose.

Rose held Hella's hand. They marched all the way to the train station where they were crammed into cars with 7,000 other Jews. This was the first transport of the day from the ghetto in 1942. I would never see them again. They were sent to Treblinka. No one came back from Treblinka.

Liquidation of the Jewish ghetto, 1943

"Ghetto A" was destroyed on March 13, 1943, and all the workers were sent to Plaszow KZ Concentration Camp. The action was personally led by SS-Untersturmführer Amon Göeth, the new commandant of the Plaszow camp. On March 14, 1943, the SS liquidated "Ghetto B." Many people were killed in courtyards and in the streets. The last remaining Jews were deported in trucks to Auschwitz-Birkenau. Several weeks after the liquidation of the ghetto, the Jewish policemen, the last members of the *Judenra*t (a council representing a Jewish community in a German- occupied territory) were sent to the Plaszow Concentration Camp.

Collecting the Jewish Property

Columns of Jewish prisoners were led back into the ghetto for the collection of Jewish property that had been left behind in the houses. This plundering continued until December 1943.

A World War II-era map of Poland

*Jews digging to the amusement of German officers,
1941-43*

*Jewish policemen used by the Germans in Krakow Ghetto and in Plaszow
Concentration Camp*

SIX

THE CONCENTRATION CAMPS

"I never expected to live past today."

The Plaszow Camp

The Plaszów, or Kraków-Plaszów Concentration Camp, was a Nazi labor camp built by the Nazis in Plaszów, a southern suburb of Kraków (now part of Podgórze district), soon after the German invasion of Poland.

The Plaszów camp was a forced labor camp that was constructed on the grounds of two Jewish cemeteries. Commanding the camp was Amon Göeth, an SS commandant from Vienna. He was known for being sadistic in the orders he issued to govern the daily treatment and extermination of prisoners. He was particularly cruel toward those who had been declared unfit for work. For them, death came as a relief.

This camp was a slave (*Arbeitslager*) or "work camp" supplying manpower to several armament factories, including that of Oskar Schindler, and also supplied workers to a stone quarry. The death rate in the camp was very high and many prisoners, including children and women, died of typhus, starvation, or execution. Individual and mass shootings were not uncommon there.

While my father, brother Nathan, and I were prisoners there, my brother was once nearly killed while I watched helplessly. On that day, Göeth was measuring a cement entrance that was intended to channel and drain water. Göeth was evaluating the entrance to determine if it was even. When he concluded based upon the way water ran down that the channel was not level, he took a club and cracked Nathan's head open. It was a terrifying moment. I wondered if this was to be the cruel and violent way my brother would die. He was bleeding badly, but lucky he survived. Göeth was angry that the water drained improperly, and for that my brother almost lost his life.

Göeth was a terror and feared by everyone, and he would find plea- sure standing on a balcony and randomly shooting Jews with his rifle. (In the movie *Schindler's List*, actor Ralph Fiennes plays Göeth with chilling accuracy and is shown relishing this ghoulish pastime.) Göeth enjoyed putting fear into the hearts of Jews while making money for himself by renting us, his Jewish slaves, to Schindler and Pilefsky an owner of a company, like Schindler, who had a deal with Göeth and used Jewish slaves and pocketing the money.

Göeth had been Schindler's friend in Krakow. I remember seeing them riding their horses, looking to see if anyone was trying to escape from the ghetto. Both of them wore guns, but Göeth was the only one that actually used his gun. If he spotted a Jew trying to escape, Göeth with a satanic smirk on his face would shoot to kill.

Entrance to Plaszow Concentration Camp, 1942, "Work Makes You Free"

Plaszow Concentration Camp, 1942

Soldiers lining up for roll call at Plaszow, 1942

Nathan Fischer (far left, second row), brother of Mayer Fischer, and a group of carpentry workers at Plaszow Concentration Camp

Plaszow Concentration Camp

Amon Göeth, Commander of Plaszow Concentration Camp, 1942

Amon Göeth, overlooking Plaszow Concentration Camp, 1943

Hanging Göeth

At war's end, the Jews hunted Göeth down. He was captured and tried. My brother Nathan was a witness against him during that trial and got his revenge on the day that Göeth was hung in the center square of the city of Krakow on September 13, 1946, by Poland's postwar communist government. Göeth's hanging was a small measure of justice for his role in killing thousands of Jews.

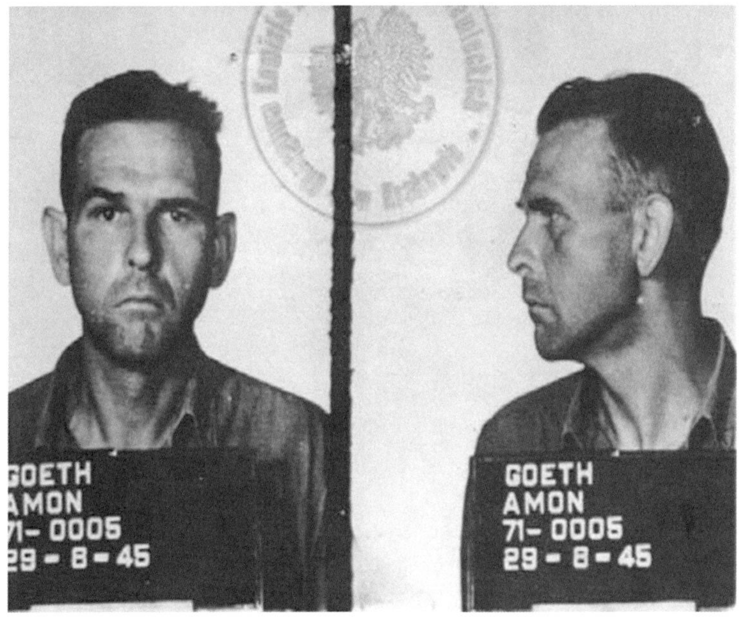

Amon Göeth photo when arrested by the Allies, 1945

The Mauthausen Camp

"My number was 84674 . . . I still remember."

After Plaszow, my friends went to Schindler's factory. I took myself off Schindler's celebrated list, because my father and brother did not make the list. I would not abandon them. I had a $20 American gold coin, which I had managed to obtain before there was a Krakow Ghetto. I originally had about ten of these coins and had somehow managed to hold on to one of them as we exited the ghetto and headed to the Plazsow Concentration Camp. I hid that coin in a piece of soap and used it to pay a clerk and arrange for my father, Baruch, brother Nathan, and I to be sent from Plazsow together to the same Mauthausen Barracks and Concentration Camp instead of being on "Shindler's List." The SS policy was generally to separate all members of the same family. Fortunately, no one knew that we were family. Thus, my father, brother, and I stayed together almost to the end.

We were all sent together to Mauthausen Concentration Camp in Austria, where were loaded into cattle car trains covered with barbwire and shipped. Every camp had a selection process when you arrived: to the right was death, and to the left was work. After our arrival at Mauthausen camp my father, brother, and I were blessedly sent to the left.

At Mauthausen Concentration Camp, we needed clothes and they gave us striped pajamas. They gave us the shoes from dead people. They had every size, yet they intentionally gave each Jew a pair of ill-fitting shoes to further humiliate us. Sometimes they were too large and sometimes they were too small. So after we got our shoes, we coordinated with other prisoners and exchanged our shoes until eventually we were able to find a pair in the correct size. There were thousands of prisoners at Mauthausen and when we could, we would help one other.

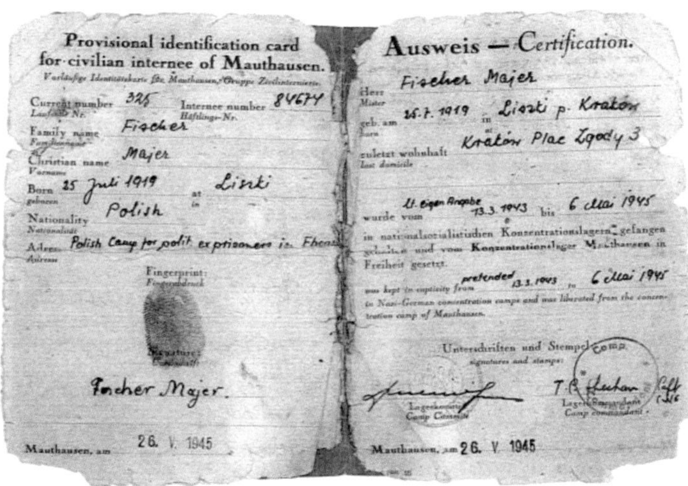

Mayer Fischer's Identification card for being a "Civilian internee of Mauthausen."
From 1943-1945

From the beginning, Mauthausen prisoners were used as forced labor either for the construction of the camp itself or for backbreaking work in the Wienergraben stone quarry. As labor became increasingly scarce, the forced labor of camp inmates became increasingly important, especially in war-related industries, and the number of prisoners incarcerated at Mauthausen and its sub-camps steadily increased. On January 1, 1945, the Mauthausen camp system had 73,351working prisoners, 959 of them women. More men were incarcerated at Mauthausen than any other concentration camp system in Nazi Germany. Mauthausen had the third largest total prisoner population, behind Buchenwald and Gross-Rosen.

On March 4, 1944, the German Armed Forces High Command (OKW) issued a decree which was dubbed the "Bullet Decree" or "Operation K," which mandated the transport of escaped and recaptured prisoners of war other than British and U.S. prisoners to Mauthausen to be shot. The decree applied to all recaptured officers and those recaptured noncommissioned officers deemed no longer capable of work. The SS imprisoned the recaptured soldiers in Barrack 20 in Mauthausen. Some were shot; others were beaten or starved to death.

The SS incarcerated more than 10,000 Soviet prisoners of war at Mauthausen. Other registered prisoners at Mauthausen included 37,000 non-Jewish Poles, 23,000 Soviet civilians, 8,650 Yugoslav civilians, 6,300 Italians, and 4,000 Czechs. By 1944 there were also forty-seven Allied military personnel: thirty-nine Dutchmen, seven British soldiers, and one U.S. soldier, all agents of the British Secret Operations Executive. The SS further transported thousands of others to Mauthausen, where they were murdered without ever being registered as prisoners in the camp.

Before May 1944, the SS incarcerated relatively few Jews at Mauthausen. The total number of Jewish prisoners between 1938 and the end of February 1944 was 2,760. Most of those were reported dead by the end of 1943. During the period from March through December of 1944, at least 13,826 Jews arrived in Mauthausen, most of whom were Hungarian and Polish Jews, and approximately 500 were women. The SS had deported virtually all of them from Auschwitz, Birkenau, and Plaszow camps to Mauthausen. In all, the SS registered 25,271 Jews in the Mauthausen camp complex. The actual number of Jews, including arrivals during the last week of the war which is when the prisoner registration process broke down may have pushed the number as high as 29,500.

Stammlager, the main Mauthausen camp, had three principal sections. Camp I was the original protective detention camp. Camp II was the camp workshop area, which was where prisoners were forced to work. The SS later converted this area to prisoner barracks in the spring of 1944. Located at the opposite side of the roll call square from Camp I was a chain of long, stone buildings that housed various camp services such as the prisoners' kitchen, showers, laundry, the bunker, and the gas chamber. Nearby stood the crematoria facilities, along with the site where the prisoners were shot.

To the west, off the entrance road to the main camp, was Camp III, the so-called infirmary camp. The SS originally constructed this facility in the fall 1941 for Soviet prisoners of war, and as a result it was frequently referred to as "The Russian Camp."

Walls and/or electrified wire surrounded the various camps. Watchtowers and SS guards surrounded the entire complex. The SS commandant's office and the barracks for the SS administrative personnel and guard units were located to the west of the camp.

It staggers the imagination to realize that 197,464 registered prisoners passed through the Mauthausen camp system between August 1938 and May 1945, and it is reported that at least 95,000 died there. More than 14,000 of these prisoners were Jewish.

Copy of a list of prisoners at Mauthausen Camp, 1945. Mayer Fischer #84674 is listed as Fischer, Majer 25-7-19, seventh line from bottom, above.

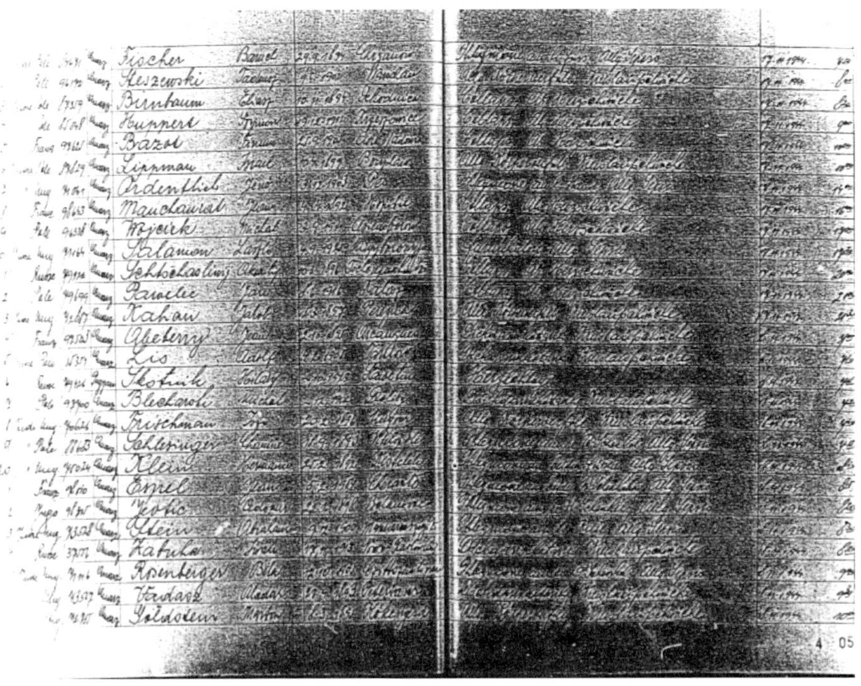

Nr.	Name	Vorname			Geburtsdatum	Ort
84651	F[illegible]	[illegible]		VT	13 [illegible]	[illegible]
84652	F[illegible]	[illegible]			[illegible]	[illegible]
84653	[illegible]	[illegible]		[illegible]	[illegible]	[illegible]
84654	[illegible]	[illegible]			[illegible] 4.[illegible]	K[illegible]
84655	Farber	R[illegible]			5 6 00	[illegible]
84656	Farber	Leon			[illegible]	[illegible]
84657	Ferenc	Mayer		[illegible]	15.4.[illegible]	[illegible]
84658	Ferenc	[illegible]ach			1[illegible] 3 21	[illegible]
84659	Fertig	[illegible]atan			11.11.[illegible]	[illegible]
84660	Feuer	Natan		VT	1.9.[illegible]	[illegible]
84661	F[illegible]	Chaim Beile			11.3.[illegible]	[illegible]
84662	Fija	Berek			[illegible].[illegible] 99	[illegible]
84663	F[illegible]	Cyper			16.6.11	Proja[illegible]
84664	F[illegible]	Abraham			5.4.21	Kra[illegible]
84665	Finder	Icek			17.5.04	Zab[illegible]
84666	Finaer	Simon			16.7.00	[illegible]
84667	Finkelstein	Chaim			3.12.[illegible]	[illegible]
84668	Finkelstein	Israel			10.12.21	Zwol[illegible]
84669	Fisch	Josef			20.12.1[illegible]	[illegible]
84670	Fisch	Abraham			1.1.15	[illegible]
84671	Fischer	Baruch			29.9.94	Elzja[illegible]
84672	Fischer	Gruta			21.[illegible].09	[illegible]
84673	Fischer	Salamon			3.11.15	[illegible]
84674	Fische	Majer			20.7.19	[illegible]
84675	Fischer	Samuel			7.6.30	Elzja[illegible]
84676	Fischer	Natan			3.12.23	B[illegible]
84677	Fischgrund	[illegible]artz			24.7.07	[illegible]
84678	Fischgrund	Moses			25.9.14	[illegible]
84679	Fischgrund	[illegible]			2.6.22	[illegible]
84680	Fischer	Edmund		N	15.2.94	Jarosl[illegible]

KONZENTRATIONSLAGER MAUTHAUSEN   Mauthausen, den 11. August 1944
    Schutzhaftlager

84301 – 88840

Liste der Zugänge vom 10. August 1944. (4 590 Juden)

1.	Abraham	Albert	28.9.07	Alsoberegzo	Schneider	84301	Ungar.
2.	Abrahamowicz	Natan	18.7.11	Wieliczka	Zimmermann	84302	Pole
3.	Abramczyk	Szulim	9.1.16	Ksiaz Wielki	Stricker	84303	"
4.	Abramowicz	Abram	1.12.08	Dabrowa G.	Schneider	84304	"
5.	Acker	Chaim	4.11.06	Jaworow	Schneider	84305	"
6.	Adelist	Dawid	24.8.14	Czestochowa	Metallarb.	84306	"
7.	Adler	Szulim	17.11.19	Kalisz	Mützenmacher	84307	"
8.	Aftergut	Naftali	8.7.25	Bochnia	Lehrling	84308	"
9.	Ajdelsztajn	Alter	16.8.12	Strozy	Tischler	84309	"
10.	Ajzenberg	Israel	29.4.10	Radom	Gärtner	84310	"
11.	Akierman	Kopel	7.9.16	Przytyk	Schuster	84311	"
12.	Aleksandrowicz	Josef	14.4.06	Krakau	Auto-Schloß.	84312	"
13.	Aleksandrowicz	Salo	21.10.08	Krakau	Schuster	84313	"
14.	Aleksandrowicz	Jerzy	27.6.25	Paris	Schäftemacher	84314	"
15.	Alper	Zygmunt	18.9.85	Jiezierzany	Bau-Techniker	84315	"
16.	Altbach	Karl	31.3.29	Drohobycz	Schneider	84316	"
17.	Altbauer	Isak	11.12.05	Drohobycz	Installateur	84317	"
18.	Alter	Jonas	10.4.23	Sokolow	Schuster	84318	"
19.	Attesländer	Josef	8.5.10	Krakau	Schuster	84319	"
20.	Attesländer	Gustaw	6.2.12	Krakau	Schuster	84320	"
21.	Altkorn	Leon	1932	Kropewnik	Schüler	84321	"
22.	Altman	Maurycy	15.7.05	Krosno	Arbeiter	84322	"
23.	Altman	Chaskiel	30.5.11	Grenau	Sattler	84323	"
24.	Alweiss	Abraham	16.4.08	Tarnow	Schneider	84324	"
25.	Ambruch	Moses	15.3.12	Drohobycz	Maler	84325	"
26.	Amsterdam	Hirsch	27.2.22	Krosno	Masch.Schloß.	84326	"
27.	Amsterdam	Naftali	1.5.23	Krosno	" "	84327	"
28.	Amsterdam	Paul	19.9.20	Wieliczka	Buchbinder	84328	"
29.	Apelbaum	Pinkus	15.10.06	Koprzywnica	Schuster	84329	"
30.	Apfelbaum	Dawid	17.6.23	Krakow	Schuster	84330	"
31.	Appel	Daniel	22.7.22	Lwow	Schloß-Lehrling	84331	"
32.	Arbus	Smul	5.11.00	Belzyce	Tischler	84332	"
33.	Argand	Herman	29.5.08	Dobromil	Buchbinder	84333	"
34.	Axonowicz	Hersz	24.4.21	Kielczyglow	Stricker	84334	"
35.	Asb	Isaak	16.1.01	Bendzin	Arbeiter	84335	"
36.	Attenländer	Moses	31.10.22	Rozwadow	Anstreicher	84336	"
37.	Ausenberg	Izrael	26.7.10	Tarnow	Schneider	84337	"
38.	Awigdor	Isak	2.1.16	Neu Sandez	Tischler	84338	"
39.	Awigdor	Abraham	12.8.26	Drohobyez	Tischler	84339	"
40.	Backenroth	Leopold	5.5.23	Rybnik	Holzmanipulant	84340	"
41.	Rachman	Berek	20.11.19	Zamosc	Schuhmacher	84341	"
42.	Bachman	Jozef	23.4.23	Boryslaw	Masch.Schloß.	84342	"
43.	Bachner	Jakob	26.7.04	Bielitz	Schneider	84343	"
44.	Backenrot	Izrael	2.9.15	Lisznia	Schuster	84344	"
45.	Backenroth	Dawid	15.11.16	Schodnica	Zimmermann	84345	"
46.	Backenroth	Henryk	27.8.20	Krakau	Zimmermann	84346	"
47.	Backenroth	Joachim	10.8.23	Schodnica	Zimmermann	84347	"
48.	Badrian	Josef	11.7.94	Krassow	Bürstenbinder	84348	"
49.	Baitel	Wolf	8.11.03	Tomaszow M.		84349	"

Nr.	Name	Vorname	geb.	Geburtsort	Beruf	Nr.	
1.	Feldinger	Moses	13.11.06	Krzapiwnik N.	Gasmonteur	84651	Pole
2.	Feldman	Wolf	17.12.22	Radom	Schuster	84652	"
3.	Felsen	Leo	8.2.13	Boryslaw	Elektromont.	84653	"
4.	Feniger	Bernard	20.4.91	Rzeszow	Buchbinder	84654	"
5.	Farber	Rubin	5.6.99	Krakau	Bürstenmacher	84655	"
6.	Ferber	Aron	1.6.04	Krakau	Stanzer	84656	"
7.	Ferenc	Majer	15.4.26	Caosowice	Klempner	84657	"
8.	Ferenc	Nonch	15.3.21	Csustowie	"	84658	"
9.	Fertig	Natan	11.11.11	Olesno	Schneider	84659	"
0.	Feuer	Nathan	1.9.04	Stanislawow	Dreher	84660	
1.	Filfus	Chaim Bela	11.3.12	Krasnik	Tischler	84661	"
2.	Figa	Berek	3.5.99	Korczyn	Schneider	84662	"
3.	Figa	Ojzer	16.6.11	Prossowiece	Schneider	84663	"
4.	Filles	Abraham	6.4.21	Krakau	Schlossergehilfe	84664	"
5.	Finder	Izak	17.5.04	Zabno	Schuster	84665	"
6.	Finder	Simon	16.7.00	Krakau	Schneider	84666	"
7.	Finkelstein	Efraim	3.12.18	Krakau	Bauschlosser	84667	"
8.	Finkelstein	Israel	10.12.21	Zwolen	Riemer	84668	"
9.	Fisch	Josef	25.12.10	Brzostek	Schneider	84669	"
0.	Fisch	Abraham	8.1.15	Tarnow	Schneider	84670	"
1.	Fischer	Baruch	29.9.94	Chrzanow	Zimmerrer	84671	
2.	Fischer	Gyula	22.6.04	Avasfeleö F.	Schneider	84672	Ungar.
3.	Fischer	Salamon	3.11.13	Drohobycz	Tischler	84673	Pole
4.	Fische	Majer	25.7.19	Liszki	Zimmermann	84674	"
5.	Fischer	Samuel	7.8.20	Chrzanow	Kürschner	84675	"
6.	Fischer	Natan	3.12.23	Brzesko	Landarbeiter	84676	"
7.	Fischgrund	Eliasz	24.7.07	Harbutowice	Schneider	84677	"
8.	Fischgrund	Moses	25.9.14	Krakau	Hilfsarbeiter	84678	"
9.	Fischgrund Emil	2.6.23		Krakau	Hilfsarbeiter	84679	"
0.	Fischler	Edmund	15.2.94	Samoklecki	Arzt Internist	84680	
1.	Fischler	Josef	10.3.23	Krakau	Zimmermann	84681	"
2.	Fieszkin	Jakob	-.1.26	Rubiezewice	Schuster Lehrl.	84682	"
3.	Fiszman	Michal	16.12.22	Radom	Schlosser	84683	"
4.	Flink	Abraham	22.3.14	Tarnow	Schneider	84684	"
5.	Flug	Chyja	28.2.26	Krasnik	Lehrling	84685	"
6.	Flug	Samul	8.7.26	Krasnik	Lehrling	84686	"
7.	Fledermaus	Alter	7.2.10	Krasnik	Tischler	84687	"
8.	Fleischer	Isak	3.4.05	Teschen	Schneider	84688	Tsch.
9.	Forat	Adolf	6.5.35	Drohobycz	Schüler	84689	Pole
0.	Forat	Jakob	23.10.06	Drohobycz	Schuster	84690	"
1.	Fürster	Natan	25.9.00	Krakau	Schneider	84691	"
2.	Fortgang	Jakob	11.3.13	Tarnow	Schneider	84692	"
3.	Frajmund	Jakub	9.4.09	Warschau	Schuster	84693	"
4.	Frank	Salamon	16.8.26	Tarnow	Sattler	84694	"
5.	Frank	Salo	15.5.27	Bielitz	Kürschnerlehrl.	84695	"
6.	Frank	Samuel	29.1.23	Nagykaroly	Landarbeiter	84696	Ung.
7.	Fränkel	Isydor	15.12.98	Schodnice	Zahnarzt	84697	Pole
8.	Fränkel	Simon	27.4.10	Krakau	Buchbinder	84698	"
9.	Fränkel	Josef	26.1.12	Krenau	Schneider	84699	"
0.	Fränkel	Aron	8.12.26	Krakau	Buchbinder	84700	"

Mauthausen Arrival

I was with my father, brother, and two cousins after we were sorted upon our arrival at Mauthausen Concentration Camp. First, we deloused in the showers, and then we got new Heflinger uniforms, with their distinctive vertical blue and black stripes. The SS took us to the quarry in Mauthausen to work on the big stones. The path to the quarry was a rugged climb totaling 183 stone steps. Each of us was tested for strength and endurance. You were told, "Pick up a stone and walk up the steps," and if you made it to the top, you lived and were sent to work. If not, you were sent to death.

I made my decision and grabbed a stone from the pile. "Any stone! Just hurry and grab a stone and run." That's what they said. All the men started grabbing stones and running.

The SS shouted, "*Schnell! Schnell*! Schell! (Fast! Fast! Fast!) You go *schnell!*"

I understood later that this was a test, to see how fit we were to work. But in that moment, I just knew that one had to react quickly, even in confusion. I grabbed the first stone I saw and I made it up to the top. When I walked up the steps there was a Ukrainian SS man in a black uniform. He shouted at me, "Why did you take such a small stone? It is too small. What are you, a little girl?"

I looked down at the stone. It looked big enough to me. I had selected it on pure impulse, paying no attention to its size or dimensions. The officer raised his gun and brought the butt down, striking me upon the head, hard.

I wasn't sure how long I had been unconscious, but it couldn't have been long or I would have been dead. I opened my eyes and felt the dust on my face and the hard, rocky earth beneath me. It was cold, and I could feel my head pulsing, like my heart was in my scalp. I realized what had happened at the same moment that I realized that I had to move again, and fast. The SS man was standing over me. I stood up, ran down the stairs, grabbed the biggest stone I saw, and I cradled it under my arm like a football. I ran back up the stairs and made it to the top. All 183 steps. When I reached the top, I passed their test. Blood was pouring down my face. They sent me to Block Barrack Number 20.

I didn't see my father and brother when they came up the steps. I was twenty-one, Nathan was sixteen, and my father was forty-four years old and in great shape for his age. We all made it somehow, and somehow, we were able to reconnect in the barracks. The blow to my head left a bump. I still have that bump on my head from that rifle butt.

Every day I believed was going to be the last day of my life. So every day I would take a risk, a risk that helped me survive.

We didn't work at Mauthausen. We just waited and waited. After about two weeks, they sent us to Melk.

KL.:

HÄftl.-Nr.: 84674   P Jude

Häftlings-Personal-Karte

Fam.-Name: Fischer   Überstellt   Personen-Beschreibung:
Vorname: Maier   am: _______ an KL.   Grösse: 167 cm
Geb. am: 25.7.19 Pinkie   Gestalt: mittel
Stand: ledig   Kinder: am: _______ an KL.   Gesicht: rund
Wohnort: Krakau   Augen: braun
Strasse: Kobierzynska 43   am: _______ an KL.   Nase: flac
Religion: mos   Staatsang.: Polen   Mund: norm
Wohnort d. Angehörigen: Vater   am: _______ an KL.   Ohren: nera
    Baruch F   Zähne: geo
    KLM   am: _______ an KL.   Haare: schwarz
Eingewiesen am: 10.8.44 KLM   Sprache: deutsch poln
durch: Dauth   Plaszow   am: _______ an KL.
in KL.:   Bes. Kennzeichen:
Grund: Pole Jude   Entlassung:
Vorstrafen: am: _______ durch KL.:   Charakt.-Eigenschaften:

mit Verfügung v.: _______   Sicherheit b. Einsatz:

Strafen im Lager:
    Grund: Art   Bemerkung: Körperliche Verfassung:

KL./Bu. 44-500 000   10512

Erlernter Beruf: zuletzt ausg. Beruf: Arbeitsbuch Nr.:
    Zimmerer   Berufsgruppe:
Ausgebildet in der Zeit
als _______ im KL

Eingesetzt
1. vom 10.8.44 bis 26.1.44 als   bei   Quarantäne
2. 26.1.44   Quer
3.
4.
5.
6.
7.
8.
9.
10.
11.
12.
13.   Nr. einw. 51729 A
14.   Haftlingsnummer in Natzweiler
15.   Org. D-Nau-30 / 5149
16.
17.
18.
19.
20.
          10513

Mayer Fischer's personal work card, #84674

Selection upon arrival at Mauthausen Concentration Camp

Selection upon arrival at Mauthausen Concentration Camp, 1943-45

Selection upon arrival at Mauthausen Concentration Camp, 1943-45

Selection upon arrival at Mauthausen Concentration Camp, 1943-45

Mauthausen Concentration Camp, 1944-45

Mauthausen Concentration Camp, 1944-45

Mauthausen Concentration Camp, 1943-45

Mauthausen Concentration Camp, 1943-45

Mauthausen Concentration Camp, 1943-45

Mauthausen Concentration Camp, 1943-45

Mauthausen Concentration Camp, 1943-45

Prisoners at the Mauthausen Concentration Camp during roll call, 1943-45. Every 10th person was shot.

Mauthausen Concentration Camp, 1943-45

Mauthausen Concentration Camp, 1943-45

Workers at Mauthausen Concentration Camp, 1943-45

Barracks at Mauthausen Concentration Camp, 1943-45

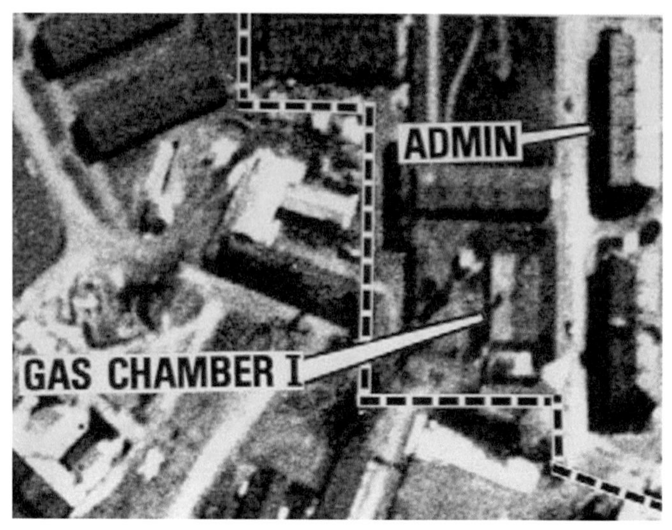

Map showing the location of the gas chamber at Mauthausen Concentration Camp, 1943-45

Quarry at Mauthausen Concentration Camp

The 183 steps at Mauthausen

Concentration Camp that all workers had to carry a stone to the top of to see if they were healthy enough to work. If they couldn't do it, they were sent to the gas chamber.

Prisoners working the quarry, Mauthausen Concentration Camp

Quarry at Mauthausen Concentration Camp, 1943-45

Mauthausen Concentration Camp after liberation, 1945

Mauthausen Concentration Camp after liberation, 1945

Prisoner conditions at Mauthausen Concentration Camp upon liberation, 1945

Prisoner conditions at Mauthausen Concentration Camp upon liberation, 1945

Barry Fischer's visit to Mauthausen Concentration Camp, 2004

Mauthausen Concentration Camp, 2004

Mauthausen Concentration Camp Museum, 2004

Mauthausen Concentration Camp Museum, 2004

Mauthausen Concentration Camp barracks, 2004

Restored interior of Mauthausen Concentration Camp barracks, 2004

Restored interior of the barracks of Mauthausen Concentration Camp, 2004

Artist's rendering of prisoners inside the barracks of Mauthausen Concentration Camp, 2004

The prisoners' bathroom at Mauthausen Concentration Camp, 2004

Memorial to those who died at Mauthausen Concentration Camp, 2004

Memorial to those who died at Mauthausen Concentration Camp, 2004

Memorial to those who died at Mauthausen Concentration Camp, 2004

"Between April 21, 1944, and April 15, 1945, a concentration camp existed in Melk. The camp was situated at the Pionierkaserne, the 'pioneer barracks.' The 14,390 prisoners deported to Melk worked on the construction of a huge subterranean tunnel between Melk and Loosdorf [a hamlet in Lower Austria]. In the tunnel, weaponry and military equipment were to be manufactured for the Steyr-Daimler- Puch AG Company. At least 4,801 prisoners died in the camp and on the building site. More than 3,500 of them were burned in the camp's crematorium erected there in the fall of 1944."

Melk, Sub-Camp of Mauthausen

I bribed a Jewish clerk working for the Germans who was in charge of selecting who would be assigned to Melk prior to being shipped from Mauthausen. I paid him with a gold coin which I had hidden from the very beginning. I held on to that coin with the hope that one day it would save our lives. And it did. My father, brother, and I were selected to go to Melk and were shipped shortly thereafter on the transport from Mauthausen.

Melk, like Mauthausen, was an all-men's camp. It was cold there, but I was always working so I never felt the cold. Sleeping conditions in the barracks were as follows: There were one hundred Jews, sleeping three in each bunk, which also helped us stay warm in the cold. There were no mattresses. We slept on wooden slats. I recall that the barracks were clean and the wood was hard. The only problem was the lice! They itched like crazy all over our bodies and scalp. We all took showers every day, but lice were still a problem. Every few months they put us all into a shower and de-loused us with some chemical. While we were in the showers we never knew if we were going to be showered with water or gassed to death.

On one occasion, when I was out after dark, waiting for a cigarette deal to go down, I saw a guard approaching. I began scratching my head furiously. The guard, thinking I had lice, changed his direction immediately!

We felt lucky because we had warm and cold water. There was no soap. I showered every day and used a very hard and abrasive substitute for soap. I don't know what it was, but we used it to help clean our bodies. We were lucky.

Every morning, the Germans gave us coffee and a piece of bread that was supposed to last the whole day. For lunch we had soup hot water with a potato in it. And in the evening, they gave us soup again. The precious bread was given to us just once a day, and if we wanted to have bread throughout the day, we had to save it from the morning's ration.

As the Germans' slaves, we prisoners were often given tasks that we knew would help the Axis alliance, but we were powerless to refuse. The Germans needed to hide their plane manufacturing plant so the Americans wouldn't bomb it. To protect the planes, we dug a deep tunnel in and under the nearby mountain, and the Germans set up and built their planes, inside the tunnel. The American bombs could not penetrate the factory at Melk, thanks to the hard work of all of us Jewish slave prisoners at the Melk Concentration Camp.

At night, I heard the sound of Allied bombs as they dropped on the City of Melk. In our barracks, stacked three high, we talked about the war, but we had no information. Praise God, the Allies never bombed our camp.

While we dug the mountain tunnel, walls would collapse when the digging was not properly done. Some prisoners were killed, and it was clear that we needed to dig properly or we would die in that tunnel. Many more accidental deaths occurred because the Germans pushed us to dig more quickly. They didn't care if we lived or died.

There was not much to be thrilled about while spending eight to ten hours a day of hard labor in the dusty innards of a mountain. But every day that I was at Melk I tried to fool the SS.

Each morning, the SS brought us into the tunnel to dig through the mountain wall. The goal was to dig eighteen inches by the end of each day. At least we had tools and weren't expected to do so with our hands. The mountain was made of shale, clay, and sand. Our shovels sometimes struck granite. After carefully measuring, an SS officer would place a spike in the floor measuring eighteen inches from the wall. I dug eighteen inches in my shift, and the guards left me alone to work. It was dusty, and they didn't want to be there because it was hard to breathe. On my first day I dug all day. The guards came and went a few times, but didn't stay long. The work was backbreaking, and there was no one to talk to or watch. The more I dug, the more I thought. In the lamp light of the tunnel, I watched my ax rise and fall, my shovel plunging into the clay. All the while I thought.

I wiped the sweat off my brow. My hands were covered with dirt. With each shovelful of rocks, I thought. I thought about that spike. I became obsessed with it. And when I stopped to wipe my forehead again, I put my shovel down. Stepping softly toward the spike, I placed both hands around it and, perhaps feeling a little like Arthur in the legend of Excalibur, I pulled the spike out of the earth. I moved the spike two feet back away from the wall in the tunnel and with the end of my shovel, hammered it back in at the same height. The SS always thought I worked hard and dug more than eighteen inches! It appeared that I had dug a full twenty-four inches, but I fooled them while I saved my strength.

With each bang the corners of my mouth twitched, but the grin quickly dissipated. I sat down and took a few deep breaths. I crossed my legs and looked up at the roof of the tunnel. I heard the sounds of far-off hammering, a trickle of water, and the sound of bat wings flapping. "But what's the difference," I thought, "whether I live or die? It's all the same." Every day I thought I was going to die. Every day could have been my last. So every day I took a risk. I took a chance. I dug less than I was supposed to. I conserved my energy. I took food from the kitchen that was controlled by the Russians. Whatever I could do to stay alive, I did it, and I shared what I could with my father and my brother.

My hearing was good, as was my eyesight, so when the SS came to check on me, I was always working. They never knew it was me who was fouling up their daily eighteen-inch quota. There were three shifts that worked in that tunnel. Jews worked all day and all night. And the Germans, who so precisely measured everything, could never figure out why their tunnel ended up short! This small victory of outwitting the Germans buoyed my spirit and gave me the strength to carry on.

Staying Alive

There were certain things you could do to stay alive and preserve your energy. Every little bit helped. If your senses were keen, then you had an advantage. My brother Nathan didn't have the sharp eyesight that I had. The Nazis had broken his glasses so he could never see if the guards were around or if anyone was coming. As a result, he nearly worked himself to death.

As a non-smoker, I had an advantage over people who smoked. Every two to four weeks I received six cigarettes as a reward for working hard. Cigarettes were the currency of choice in the camp, and I traded them for bread. The deals always went down behind the barracks, in the shadows. The guys who worked in the kitchen or who had gotten a portion of bread with their meal that day would tuck it into their shirt and hand it to me. This was another way I stayed alive. I never thought that one day I would make my living in America selling cigarettes. (In the camp I exchanged them for food, but in Brooklyn Nathan and I owned Rogers Tobacco, Candy and Stationery and were wholesale cigarette distributors who would sell cigarettes to candy stores.) Every day I wondered if I would make it past today.

I never gave up. I always had a strong will to live. I was even jealous of the birds, flying in and out of the camp, particularly when we were in Ebensee Concentration Camp. The birds could fly in and fly out. I could not. I felt that if I survived, we would beat the Germans. The Jewish people still live today. They could not destroy us.

There is a phrase in Polish: "*Tag Mague.*" It means, "What's the difference?" So, what's the difference if you are going to die?

When the war broke out, the Russians had a fifth column of spies that were in civilian clothes and hidden. They moved among the occupied countries and were present in Poland and Austria. When the Germans caught the Russians, they were shipped to concentration camps, including Melk. In our camp they shared a barracks with us, and there were about sixty of them. They stuck together, and they didn't want to talk to anyone. But I was likeable, and I was Polish. A close ethnic cousin to the Russians, they spoke to me.

Those Russians were also in charge of the kitchen and controlled the food. The Russians would allow me to take food from the kitchen and share it with my brother and father.

One day, a German guard gave me a reward for doing something helpful around the camp. The guard gave me a pot of soup and some extra bread. I carefully carried the bowl of soup back to our bunk because I wanted to share it with my brother and my father. The problem was, I had to leave for work detail and there was no time. So I decided to hide the soup in our bunk. I told my father to have some soup and then save some for Nathan and me. Such simple pleasures were rare. The concentration camp experience broke you down to your weakest existence. My father was so hungry that he ate all of the soup. When I returned, he said he was sorry, but that he could not control himself because he was so hungry.

My father loved my brother and me. We all loved each other. We would each do whatever it took to save the other. But in that moment, he was so weak. At that time I was twenty-three. Nathan was eighteen. One day, my father was on a different shift, and I was unable to watch over him. I was unable to protect him.

Baruch Fischer Dies in Melk

My father had been knee-deep in water, digging all day. His job was to dig the gutter for the water to drain out of the pit, but the sand would hold it back. He had to push the water with a small shovel, which was an impossible task. He would move some sand and then the water would push through. The sand fell back in, over and over, and the water would not drain. During this time, my father would stand there, with one foot in the water to brace himself. His fingers were sore, his foot was swollen, and he would work like that for eight hours straight.

During one of these shifts, another worker accidently hit my father's leg with a shovel. His leg was bleeding and he couldn't walk. He was brought back to the barracks in a wheelbarrow. I was at work and I didn't know. Maybe, just maybe, I might have saved him, but it was too late. He was on his way to his death.

My father straightened his back, holding the shovel to balance himself as he climbed out of the pit, limping. He knew there was an infirmary and he had to decide quickly. He was tired. Of course they would want him to be fit for work. Perhaps they would even give him a couple of days off. A man working just outside came over to help my father, steadying his hand.

"Tell my sons I went to the infirmary," my father informed the man. "I will meet them later. I will see them soon."

I came back from work and did not find my father, so right away I asked the *blockmeister* where he was. A *blockmeister* was a Jew appointed to be in charge of a room of bunk beds as a liaison to the Germans. He reported on Jews when something went wrong. I took off running when I heard he was on his way to the infirmary. If I could catch him, I could stop him. I knew they were not taking care of people there. I knew they were killing them if they were unfit for work.

They let me into the room to see my father, but I had to be quick.

He was lying on a board when I came in. "Father?" I said softly as I walked over.

My father Baruch opened his eyes and smiled. "Mayer," he said warmly.

I took his hand and asked, "How do you feel?" "I feel better. See my foot?"

"What did they give you?"

"They gave me an injection. I feel better."

I looked at my father and I knew. I knew that they had injected him not with medicine, but with gasoline. I knew he was going to die, but I didn't tell him. I didn't know what to do, so I found Nathan and the rabbi.

"Our father is dead," I said, fighting back tears. "Within three hours he'll be dead. What should we do?"

I still blame myself for not being able to stop my father in time, before he went to the infirmary.

I found a wheelbarrow and placed my father's body in it. I knew where they dropped the bodies, so I pushed the wheelbarrow to the crematorium with a heavy heart. Jews did not often carry the bodies of other Jews around the camp unless they were ordered to do so, so the SS soldier at the crematorium questioned me when I arrived. I balanced the weight of my father in the wheelbarrow, trying to appear emotionless.

"I saw the body of this man on the ground and I thought he would start to stink," I lied. "So I brought him here to get the body out of the way."

The guard was pleasantly surprised by my initiative, and not knowing it was my father, he gave me a pot of soup as a reward for taking the extra care.

Actual crematorium where Mayer Fischer took Baruch Fischer after he had been murdered.

I took the soup back to Nathan in our barracks. And with this pot of soup, we celebrated—our father was free from pain. He was released from this life. We ate quietly, celebrating and mourning.

It was 1944, and a year before we would be liberated. We were to spend two years at the Melk camp.

When the camp was finally liberated by the U.S. troops on May 5, 1945, the SS guards fled, leaving the camp in an unbelievable situation. The dead and dying were scattered all over the grounds. The final prisoner count showed a population of over 14,000.

The Commandant of Melk was SS-Obersturmbannführer Julius Ludolf. He was hanged in April 1947.

Prisoners after liberation, Melk Concentration Camp, 1945

Prisoners at the time of liberation, Ebensee Concentration Camp, May 7, 1945

Allies liberating Melk Concentration Camp, 1945

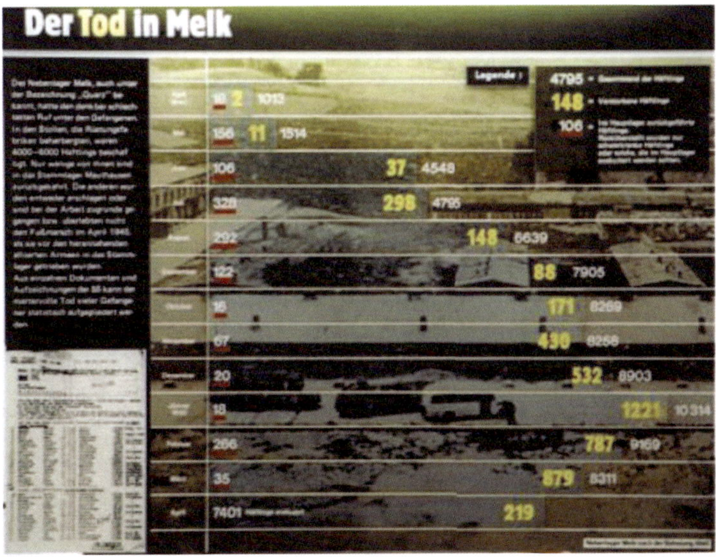

Chart showing where the prisoners in the Melk Concentration Camp came from, 2004.

From Barry Fischer's trip to the city of Melk, 2004. View of Melk, Australia, from the gate of the concentration camp. Building is city hall government building

Barbed wire fence surrounding the Melk Concentration Camp, 2004. The camp is closed to the public

The Melk prisoner population was always constant. It stayed at 20,000. Every month 2,000 new Jews came, and every month 2,000 died. The Germans always kept the workforce constant so they could get their precious tunnel dug. The Germans were desperate because the allies were bombing all the factories, leaving nowhere to build airplanes but underground.

When the Germans brought in a few thousand Jews from Budapest, within a few weeks 60 percent of them were dead. For some reason, the transports from Budapest could not take the extreme hardship, the cruel punishment, or the lack of food. They were unable to work and unable to dig. They came from the city and didn't have skills. But when shipments of Jews came from Poland, those workers lasted longer. They were able to handle the cruelty and hardship longer.

Most people do not identify "Melk" in Austria as a Killing Center, but it was one of the mainstay camps in the Mauthausen System. Melk, Mauthausen, Ebensee, Guzen, and the Castle Hartheim were linked in a monstrously cruel system of death and slavery.

The main purpose of Melk was to provide forced labor for the various tunneling projects in the surrounding hills. The hills consisted of fine sand and quartz and a vast number of prisoners were buried alive beneath the many cave-ins.

The inmates of the camp were of all nationalities. No single nationality was dominant. There were Poles, Hungarians, Yugoslavs, French, Italians, and Czechs.

A gas chamber was built and well-camouflaged. The chamber was actually better built and planned than the one at Mauthausen. It was built of brick with double walls 25 cm. apart. The inner walls were tiled like a bathroom. The double walls acted as soundproofing, so that the screams of the dying were not heard by passing prisoners or by the general public.

Melk also had its own crematorium. Its tall smokestack, pointing like a finger to the sky, was an obvious landmark. It covered a large area, and its design was an improvement over those at Mauthausen, Goshen, and Ebensee. Adjoining the crematorium was a mortuary, which was well-ventilated and well-tiled. This is where I had taken my father's body.

The village of Melk overlooked the Melk Concentration Camp. All of the civilians knew what was happening.

The Melk camp was established within the bounds of a large Wehrmacht garrison, on an Army base. Thus, it was exposed to passing soldiers and civilians. In fact, it was quite possible to look down on the camp and adjoining army barracks from the link roads, which were on a higher level. The crematorium entrance faced straight onto one of the main Wehrmacht roads. Nothing was done to conceal the stench and atrocities. The town folk and soldiers knew what was going on at Melk.

Ebensee

The Germans moved us from Melk to Ebensee by boat on the Danube River, which connected Melk and Ebensee. Ebensee was not a work camp. It was an extermination camp. The Germans wanted to kill us all, but they simply ran out of time. Liberation came for us on May 5, 1945, three and a half months after the liberation of Auschwitz by the Red Army.

I don't know how the Russians did it, since they were prisoners with us in Ebensee, but they had a radio in the camp. There was one officer among them, but since they were captured without uniforms, the Germans did not know which one was the officer. The Germans would torture them individually, but the Russians never gave up their officer. During the war, the Russians (who, as a people, impressed me as having a great lust for life) would dance energetically, squatting and kicking out their legs, and sing festive Russian songs while they lived in the block to keep up their spirits. As I recall, one of them played a harmonica quite well.

We didn't work in Ebensee. This was a *finuchtung* camp: a camp to finish us off. The Germans gave us very little food. We were there only three months until Dwight D. Eisenhower's (he was the Supreme Commander of the Allied Expeditionary Forces in Western Europe) Great American Tanks rolled into the camp.

The Russians were to the east and the Americans and supporting Allies were to the West. The dividing line between them was the Danube River. We heard the Russians approaching. We heard the bombing and the cannons. It all sounded like it was within miles of the camp. The Germans were ordered to kill all of us, but the Russians and Allies rushed to liberate Melk and Ebensee.

Within a few days the number of Germans guarding us dwindled. One day, two of the sixty Russians were discovered to be missing. They had escaped, and within a couple of days one of them returned in his officer's uniform, with two bullet belts crisscrossing his chest, which was full of shiny medals. Carrying a machine gun, he was proud to come back and liberate his remaining fifty-eight comrades. Reunited, they danced and sang Russian songs with their typical lust for life.

When the Russian soldier returned, he looked at me and said hello, acknowledging my presence. I felt proud to have been acknowledged in this way.

Doorway to a concentration camp's showers for delousing. You never knew if you would be showered with water or gassed.

View of the village of Melk from the Concentration Camp, 2004. The citizens of Melk knew what was going on inside the camp, for the Melk Concentration Camp was clearly visible to the entire

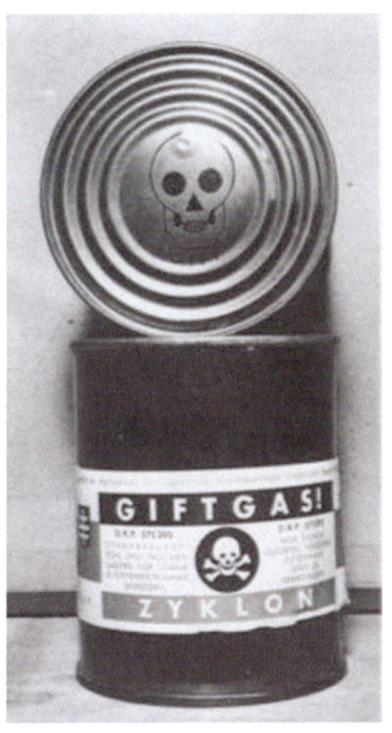

Canister of Zyklon gas. This was the gas that was used in the gas chambers.

Entrance to Melk Concentration Camp, 2004

Crematorium smokestack, Melk Concentration Camp, 2004

Melk Concentration Camp commemorative plaque, 2004

Memorial photos inside the room that housed the crematorium, 2004.

Inside the room that house the crematorium

Underground tunnels built by prisoners so the Germans could build their planes, 1945.

Memorials inside the room that housed the crematorium

For the Allied forces Steyr-Daimler-Puch was a high priority target due to the fact that the company produced armaments essential for the war effort like ball bearings, aircraft engines, and tanks.

Despite "employing" several million foreign civilian laborers and prisoners of war, the shortage of labor in the German war economy became drastic towards the end of the war. Therefore the construction of underground facilities was only feasible if concentration-camp prisoners were "employed" in large numbers.

In 1944 Steyr-Daimler-Puch began to shift its production facilities to subterranean tunnels. In Roggendorf, a small village between Loosdorf and Melk, an underground armaments factory with the code name "Quartz" was erected, originally planned with a length of 14 kilo- meters. Concentration camp prisoners were assigned to construct the underground facilities and therefore, in April 1944, a concentration camp was established in Melk.

At the time, the NS-leadership were only interested in keeping up the arms production. In contrast to this, Steyr-Daimler-Puch saw the end of the war approaching and planned to secure essential production facilities for the post-war period. The concentration camp prisoners were working in the underground tunnels and their toil resulted in the company's later interest.

SEVEN

LIBERATION

On the first of May 1945 we heard rumors around the camp that the Russians were coming. Then we heard it was the Americans who were coming to liberate us. The Russian prisoners in the camp kept me informed about what was happening on the outside.

The Russians were clever. I liked them. Somehow, they built radios and hid them. At night they picked up an AM frequently and got the news on the war. So, I knew that the war was nearing an end. One night the Russians were dancing and singing, and because I wasn't sleeping, I started singing with them. This was when they got the news that the war was over. On May 3, 1945, I woke up in the morning to go to work and realized that there were no guards. Initially there was some chaos, but mostly everyone in the camp just sat around, wondering what to do.

Prisoners at the Melk Concentration Camp upon liberation

I went to the front gate. There were no guards there, just an old man with a gun. He looked like he was one of the prisoners. I asked the old man, "Will you shoot me if I go out?"

The man said, "No."

The Germans had told him to sit there with the gun and shoot anyone who left, but he said he would not shoot me. The man didn't think the Germans were coming back, but he sat there just the same.

Without a second's hesitation, I scooted out of the gate and took the road to a nearby house. I needed food for my brother. I was wearing the threadbare striped uniform of a prisoner, and I was emaciated, almost skeletal. When I came to the house, a run-down shack with an outhouse, I knocked on the door and asked for food. The woman at the door appeared frightened. She spoke German. Finally, I understood that she wanted to know if I was going to kill her.

I gestured to my mouth and emaciated belly. "Food," I said. I knew she did not have much food herself, but she gave me a loaf of bread. I thanked her and she quickly closed the door.

I ran back to the camp, stealing a chicken from another house and breaking its neck. The old man was no longer at the gate when I returned. I saw a few others venturing out on the road.

In the barracks, Nathan lay in bed. He had lost the will to live just the night before.

"The Germans are gone. The war is over," I told him.

"I don't believe it," he groaned.

"It's true."

"I won't believe it until I see bread."

"It's right here."

I showed him the bread I'd brought back. Nathan looked at it without expression. His eyes were glassy, and he was too tired to reach for it.

"And a chicken. Look!" I stuck out the dead chicken like a trophy.

Nathan didn't answer. He was about to die.

He couldn't eat.

I broke off a piece of bread for him and told him to eat it. I found a pot and boiled the chicken over a campfire. For three days I nursed my brother back to health.

Most of the other people in the camp now went out in search of food, but all came back in the evening to sleep because they had nowhere else to go. The only clothes they had were their striped uniforms. Some whispered questions and wondered what to do next. Sometimes we all sat in complete silence. For the first time, we could hear the sound of birds singing merrily in the trees, oblivious to the unspeakable horrors that man had wrought here upon his fellow man.

Then, on May 6, the day that would be known as Liberation Day, Eisenhower's army arrived with tanks and officially liberated us. They told us we could stay or go, and that they would give us a place to stay in the barracks.

Two days later, American tanks came with boxes of clothes and canned food. It was American food, which we were not used to food such as SPAM, the popular canned meat product beloved by American GIs. Some people ate too much and died as a result. I knew better than that.

I stayed a few days in the camp and then, with Nathan and hundreds of other prisoners, we walked through the streets of Ebensee, protesting. We wanted a room and a place to sleep.

Eventually, we decided to leave that part of the country and got on the train to make our way to Linz, Austria. We didn't have any money, but as displaced persons we could ride the train for free. In Linz, there was a Displaced Persons Camp, where many of the Jews were going.

Thus began our exodus to Linz.

The liberation of Ebensee Concentration Camp by the Allies, 1945

Prisoners at Ebensee Concentration Camp following liberation, 1945

Following the liberation of Ebensee Concentration Camp, 1945

Allied liberation of Ebensee Concentration Camp, 1945

Ebensee Concentration Camp following liberation, 1945

Liberation of Ebensee Concentration Camp, 1945. The wagon is stacked with the corpses of poor souls that didn't make it out alive.

Ebensee Concentration Camp following liberation, 1945

Liberation of Ebensee Concentration Camp, 1945

Liberation by the Allies, 1945

EIGHT

DISPLACED PERSONS CAMP

In the Displaced Persons Camp in Linz, I was lucky. I had a Displaced Person (DP) card. This meant I could use public transportation and was permitted to go into stores. There were very limited supplies, but I could get what we needed. With the DP card, I could take the train across the bridge to the Russian side. I could purchase Russian wristwatches and travel with them. I could sell them to the German people and bring back the cash. We had a lot of cash! After liberation, we began to have money, clothes, a car, a chauffeur, a maid, and a bombed-out apartment building, which we took as our own. We were getting stronger, and we were free. No one was going to tell my brother and I what we could do anymore. The reign of terror was over. Now the Germans would begin to pay us back for the horrors they inflicted upon us.

Thousands of Jews didn't have homes, and many of them didn't want to return to their hometowns and cities because of the ghosts that would haunt them there. We stayed in a place called Bindermichel, which was the name of the Displaced Persons Camp in Linz Austria.

About Displaced Persons Camps

Even in the midst of the war years, The Allied powers anticipated that a refugee crisis would follow the defeat of Nazi Germany. As early as 1943, Allied forces began drafting plans to meet the challenge of liberating, rehabilitating, and repatriating the millions of displaced persons (DPs) who would come under Allied control. This colossal relief effort between May and December 1945 included the military and civilian rescue teams of the United Nations Relief and Rehabilitation Administration (UNRRA).

Bindermichl Community. Displaced Persons Camp/Community in Linz, Austria

Bindermichl Community. Displaced Persons Camp/Community in Linz, Austria

From 1945 to 1952, more than 250,000 Jewish DPs lived in camps and urban centers in Germany, Austria, and Italy. The concerns of Jewish DPs in the years following the Holocaust were problems of daily life in the DP camps, Zionism, and emigration.

Soon after liberation, survivors began searching for their families. UNRRA established the Central Tracing Bureau to help us locate relatives who had survived the concentration camps. Public radio broadcasts and newspapers contained lists of survivors and their whereabouts. The attempt to reunite families went hand-in-hand with the creation of new ones; there were many weddings and many births in the DP camps.

Schools were established and teachers came from Israel and the United States to teach the children in the DP camps. Orthodox Judaism also began its rebirth as *yeshivot* (religious schools) were founded in several camps. Religious holidays became major occasions for gatherings and celebrations. Jewish volunteer agencies supplied religious articles for everyday and holiday use.

In the DP camps, everyone was looking for someone. The Red Cross and several Jewish organizations were helping. They took names and had a system in place to connect people. Everyone asked everyone if they knew so-and-so, if they had seen them alive, and where they had seen them.

Neither my mother nor my younger sister made it. They were killed in Treblinka, but I had it on the word of a cousin that Lydia, my older sister, was still alive. I was able to call her in Krakow because she had left her phone number with the Red Cross. She had gone back to Krakow and was teaching kindergarten. I called and told her I would come right away.

I showed my DP card on the train and there was no fare. When I got to Krakow, I moved quickly through the neighborhoods, trying not to notice things that were familiar or unfamiliar, what was gone, or what was still there but not at all the same.

I finally found her with distant relatives of a friend. Our reunion was tearful. I was so happy to see my sister. It was a miracle that we survived. I could never forget it was Lydia's husband who had saved my life, but he was gone now. And Lydia, my older sister, who walked with a limp from childhood, had somehow made it through all of the selection processes at Auschwitz.

After hugging and talking, I told her that she should come with me to Linz, Austria. The DP camps were nice. It was a fresh start. They had food. And so Lydia and I left Krakow for the last time. I never, ever wanted to return to Krakow.

Lydia Wolf, Mayer Fischer's sister, in 2000 Meeting Blima

Six months after I came to Linz, a girl named Blima showed up in the apartment of a friend. There she was such a cute, pretty thing. Small and scared yet determined. She said she was looking for her father. I felt sorry for her. She was ironing her dress and had a small bundle lying on the floor.

She talked about her family. She was careful with the iron and with her dress. I noticed her voice was shaking, but she was careful to hold it in. She must be lonely, I thought. I couldn't help but remember my own sister and mother. I knew they were dead but couldn't help but wonder if my favorite Aunt Helen wasn't out there somewhere, ironing a shirt.

"Are you hungry?" Blima asked me, smiling shyly. "You must be hungry. Hans will make you food. I'll make sure you have what you need."

Blima smiled and our eyes met, and perhaps we both trusted each other. After that, I couldn't get her smile and those eyes out of my mind. I took Hans aside that night and told him to make a good dinner.

Blima Fischer, 1949

Blima Fischer, 1949

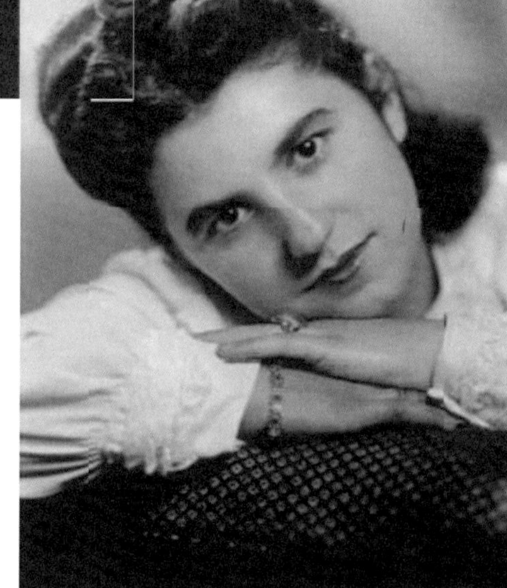

Blima Fischer, 1949

Blima Fischer, 1949

Blima Fischer, 1949

Blima Fischer, 1981

Blima and I courted briefly, and I did everything to make sure she was happy. We both liked classical music, so during our courtship we went to concerts and walked the streets of Linz. When I asked her to marry me, she said yes. We were married on June 12, 1946. I wanted to make sure she had everything she needed, and I did, for the next sixty-five years.

When Blima and I were dating, we were living in a bombed-out building with my brother Nathan, and a dear friend, Rumik Friedner. He was from Krakow and later went to serve in the Israeli Air Force, fighting for Israel's independence. Rumik Sr., our friend's father, was a goldsmith in Krakow.

During our dating period, our German employee would cook for us. We had food. The first floor of the house was good, but the top of the house was bombed-out. The owner had abandoned the building. We were beginning to have life again, to live again, and to breathe.

Emigration

After liberation, the Allies were prepared to repatriate all Jewish DPs to their homes, but many of us refused. We felt unable to return to our homeland. The memories were just too painful. The American diplomat

W. Averell Harriman, in his August 1945 report to President Harry S. Truman, recommended mass population transfer from Europe, and resettlement in British-controlled Palestine or in the United States. The report influenced President Truman to order that preference be given to DPs, especially widows and orphans, in U.S. immigration quotas. This is what allowed my family to emigrate to the United States of America.

Thank you, Harry Truman!

Truman alone could not raise restrictive U.S. immigration quotas, but he was a shrewd strategist and found a solution. On May 14, 1948, the United States and the Soviet Union recognized the state of Israel. Congress also passed the Displaced Persons Act in 1948, authorizing 200,000 DPs to enter the United States. Only a certain number of persons from each country were allowed to emigrate to the United States of America, but Truman persuaded Congress to declare displaced persons as citizens of "No Country." There was no quota limit for displaced persons. This is how we were allowed to come to America.

President Truman opened the door for us. He welcomed us to America, where we would live the rest of our lives.

Blima and Mayer Fischer, 1947

Blima Fischer, 1947

Blima Fischer, 1948

Blima Fischer, 1948

Blima and Mayer Fischer, June 6, 1949, on our wedding day1948

June 6, 1949, on our wedding day Blima would light the candles every Friday night for Shabbat in our home. We dated for four or five months, and then married. My wife was always hopeful that she would find her father. She hoped and hoped, until one day a mutual friend reported that he saw the Germans kill her father when he was taken from Bendina, their hometown just outside of Krakow. Her mother and sister were taken to Madanek and murdered. My mother and sister were shipped to and killed at Treblinka. Gone, all of them gone. All of our combined families were gone. They were sent to the showers, the doors were closed, and they were gassed to death.

Before the war, I had nine sets of aunts and uncles. The Weinstocks, who had a wine factory, had two brothers who survived, Yosak and Heshak, one of the Lieblichs' and Felchers' two brothers. We lost twenty other cousins. Eight out of our family survived. We lost forty close relatives: my parents and my sister, seven aunts and uncles, and twenty cousins. The survivors were me, Nathan, Lydia, Yosak Weinstock, Heshak Weinstock, Jacob Lieblich, and Harry and Joseph Felcher. All of my aunts and uncles were killed except one, my Aunt Helen, who we called Cha Cha. She was a great, loving person. She ended up living in Toronto and married a gentleman named Henry Turner. She then moved to Israel, where she lived out the rest of her life in Netanya, Israel. Some of their children survived. I only had five cousins that survived the war.

I had the pleasure of watching my Aunt Cha Cha enjoy my children in Brooklyn, New York. Cha Cha visited us in Brooklyn three to four times, including when my son Barry was ten, and then again for his bar mitzvah when he was thirteen. Barry traveled to Toronto to visit my Aunt Cha Cha and her husband. I was so proud that my family continued to live, continued to have life!

And so life began to be good for us in Linz. Blima and I eventually moved to Frankfurt, where we awaited the birth of our first child. Blima grew round and heavy. I marveled at her fertility. She brought home bags of ripe fruit from the market, and new colorful fabrics, which she fashioned in what I believed to be new and unique ways to fit her expanding form. I watched as she knitted very small articles of clothing. When I brought home more yarn, she responded with delight.

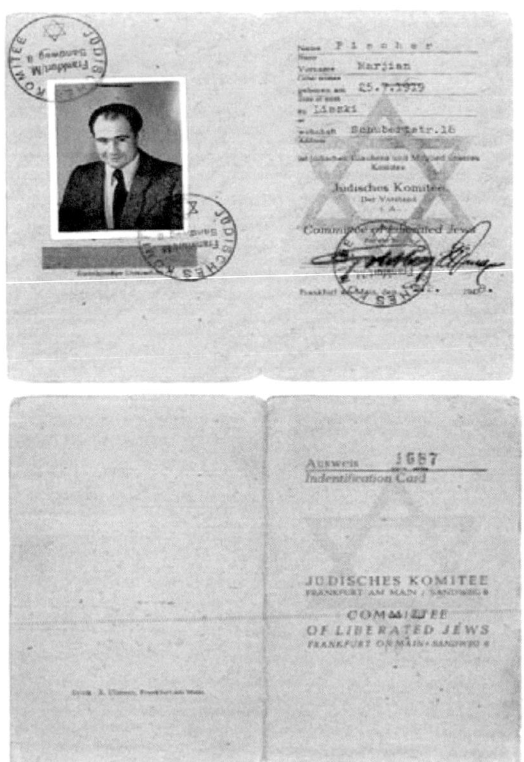

Mayer Fischer's membership card. The Committee of Liberated Jews, 1949

I have to tell you Blima's story. Blima was an extraordinary partner in life, and it was only because I was with Blima that we created such a beautiful family. We were together for sixty-four years and were married for sixty-two years. She passed away on November 6, 2009, as a result of pancreatic cancer. She was the love of my life.

You will not believe the terror that Blima experienced. It is best to hear her tell it, in her own words. The only time she ever shared the entire story, in full, living memory, was with an interviewer from the Shoah Foundation, which was founded by filmmaker Steven Spielberg in 1994 to record video testimonies of survivors of the Holocaust. *Thank you, Mr. Spielberg!*

The following is a transcript of Blima's interview:

"I was born on September 28th, 1924. We were a traditional Jewish family. My mother's name was Anja, or Anna in English. My father's name was Zindel. My father used to go to shul Friday night and Saturday. My parents were very young people. I was the oldest of three children. I had a younger brother and sister. It was a very happy home. We had a very good family life. My parents tried to give us the best that they could. They were very much into the Jewish culture, Jewish theater, and they tried to get as much out of life as they could, and our life was very happy.

"My grandmother lived very close by. I had quite a few aunts and uncles. It was a big family. So was my father's, quite a big family. But my father and his family lived in Dunbrovak, the neighboring town, not in Benjin.

"Holiday times we spent at home, together with grandmother and my mother's part of the family, because we were very close. My grand- mother was like a mother to me. Her name was Tamara and was a beautiful, hardworking woman. She was widowed very young, was left with a few children who were not married and carried on a bakery. I loved her. I did, very dearly.

"I went to a school which was primarily Jewish and most of the teachers were Jewish. The principal of the school was Jewish, and I don't remember in my class whether there was a Christian child. I don't remember. I think we were all Jewish children. And we went through the process like normal children. We went to school in the morning, came back from school. There were all kinds of activities. Wintertime, I used to go crazy and ice skate every day after school, every day. I ran home from school, got my ice skates, and went to the ice rink at a different school. I would skate for two hours, sometimes for three. Then I would go home, do homework, and do other things in the evening. I went through public school until the seventh grade, and I had a year of business school. I wanted to learn a trade to be a designer, a fashion designer, and a dressmaker. But the Germans came and war broke out.

"When I was a little older, we used to get together in a young Zionist movement with friends, both boys and girls. We used to learn a little bit about Palestine, about the settlements, the early settlements, in Palestine.

"The organization that I belonged to was HaNoar HaTzioni, and we used to meet during the spring in May, mostly in May. It was called Myupka. We used to meet early in the morning for picnics, and when we went on a picnic like this, people would bring their children. Youngsters came from neighboring towns, and we would get together and dance, sing, and learn Hebrew songs. We had a very carefree, a very happy life. And this was our life, until Hitler came, then it all shattered.

"My parents had a small shoe factory, which was developing very nicely, and we used to manufacture house slippers for ladies, house slippers for men, and summer shoes in the summer.

And it was devel- oping very, very nicely. As a matter of fact, during the war, we were doing the same thing for the Germans all working for the shoe factory that made shoes for the Germans. The whole family had papers that [documented] we all were occupied by this firm. They called these papers arbeiter (in English it means worker or laborer), and we were sending the shoes to the German army.

"We were able to sustain ourselves till 1943. Plus we weren't caught in the street somewhere, when the SS truck came and rounded up people like cattle and sent them away to the camps. And we used to hide out during the nights many, many times. If we knew, if we found out or we got wind that there was going to be a roundup, nobody slept at all. We tried to hide, tried not to get caught, for as long as we were able to. But there came a time that we weren't able to hide anymore.

"Things starting to get bad immediately, immediately. The first day we had a very bad experience. We lived in a courtyard where there were many houses, and it connected from one street to another. It was going in from one street, going through and toward the next, and the front of the building had, like a big gate. Normally, before the war, when we went out, that gate was closed at ten o'clock at night. If you came afterwards, the super had to come and unlock the gate to let you in to come home, and you had to give him a few cents for doing that for you.

"But during the war, right when the Germans came in, I would say the first week, they imposed a curfew. At 8:00 p.m. everyone had to be at home. No Jew was allowed to be in the street after 8:00 p.m. If a Jew was caught outside after eight o'clock, he didn't make it. He didn't make it.

"The first experience that we had, as I experienced, in that court- yard, was when the Germans came in, when they were marching in September first. Some of them were walking, you know, along with the big trucks. We were watching, and they looked probably into the court, and they saw a man with a beard coming from the other side.

One of the Germans started searching. We were all in a shelter, hiding, when the Germans were marching through. There must have been two hundred or more people hiding in one space. When this soldier saw that there was a Jew with a beard going somewhere, the soldier went into the courtyard and watched where the Jew was going. Naturally, he was going to the shelter to join everybody else.

"The German soldier went and followed him and found a few hundred people. He began pulling everyone out and lining everybody up in front of the building. And they started making fun of the people with the beards, and of their attire, the people with the coats. So at first the Germans were making fun, and we were very scared because this was our first experience with them. They just marched in. We knew that war was coming, but we didn't know that it was that near.

"After quite a while, they told the women and the children to go back, and they took away all the men. The men were out until the evening. By the evening, they started slowly coming back. We never thought, we never, never thought that they were going to come back. There was such hysteria and such screaming and such crying, because nobody knew whether these men were going to come back. These were fathers and brothers, grandfathers, and uncles.

"But towards the evening, they started coming back. Not in a group, but one by one, and each had a different experience. They said that the Germans spread them apart through the city. They didn't do anything to anybody. They didn't beat anybody. They let them come back. This was the first experience that I had when the Germans came.

"My second experience was a few days later, after they already imposed a curfew. They burned the synagogue. We saw the flames from the synagogue coming, and we couldn't get out. So we were standing and we were watching. It was September. It wasn't very dark yet at 8:00 p.m. We were watching the flames. We didn't know what was happening, but we knew that the synagogue was burning. We were screaming, crying. There was nothing we could do. We all congregated inside the courtyard and talked about it. There was nothing we could do. We couldn't go out into the street. We weren't allowed.

"The next day we found out that not only had the synagogue been burned, but that many of the surrounding houses had also been burned. There were a few hundred people that had tried to escape the fire, but they were shot. We saw their bodies lying around in the street.

"And after that, every day, every day of the German occupation was a different experience, every day. They used to send out trucks with the black SS, in black uniforms, and they would round up a truckload of people. We didn't know where they were taking them. They just took them away.

"So life was very scary during that time. During the day we worked. We were occupied. In the evenings we used to see friends, but ten minutes to 8:00 PM or a quarter to 8:00 pm, you saw everybody running home.

"They established a Jewish Police to watch over the people. So first you had to go through the Jewish Police and many of the boys weren't very nice either. They were trying to collaborate with the Germans. Whatever the Jewish Police didn't do, the Germans did.

"The Jewish Police carried out all kind of things. For instance, if the Germans wanted people, if they needed people, they would send out the Jewish Police to round up people at night, and the Germans did the rest. The Germans started setting up camps and sending people into them. Evidently, they needed people to work, so the Germans would grab people in the streets and send them out to the camps.

"I was working in the factory with my parents until I went away to the camp. That was in 1943. The shoe factory that my parents had was an official factory. We had forty-five people working, and we were working for the German government, for the German army. I had a certificate, a paper, it was called a *zunder.* No special consideration came with it though. But until 1943 they evidently needed what we were producing. They needed it. When they started to clear out the Jews from the area, everything stopped. Everything stopped.

"I'm forgetting the most important thing. They needed housing for the Germans. So from the main streets of the town, the Germans sent out the Jews. They took over the homes of Jews because the Germans needed quarters where they could live. So slowly, slowly they sent the people out from the streets that the Germans wanted to occupy. Wherever there was an empty apartment or wherever someone had a big apartment, they had to take in a second family or even a third family. The Jews all had to squeeze in together. Slowly the Germans started building the ghetto. It wasn't a complete ghetto at that time, yet, but later on the Germans started to concentrate Jews more and pushed people closer together, into a ghetto.

"My family and I lived across the street, a little farther down where they'd left for the Jews, in the back of the buildings. They gave us quarters because there was access, so as to not come out to the front street. There was access to the different streets because the main streets they occupied; the Jews weren't allowed to walk there. We had to put on the white armbands with the star, with the Jude, the Star of David, and this was our identification. We couldn't walk on the streets, not even during the day. We were not allowed to walk in the streets where the Germans occupied, only in the streets which were designated for the Jews.

"The food also started to get more minimal. We weren't able to buy food like we did normally, and things started to be not very good. If you had some people that you knew, some Poles that you knew, you were able to buy something from them, and they used to help a little bit, in the beginning. Then later things started getting bad. There wasn't enough food to go around. The Germans gave us coupons, so much and so much per family, and each time it was less and less. Times weren't very good during the occupation.

"And life went on like this until the end of October 1942. There was an order, and the Germans took us out on the football field and closed us up. They closed us up, the whole city.

"There was an order written and pasted all through the city that this and this day, everybody had to come to the boys' school, Hakowa. And I would say that 99 percent of the population in Benjin was on that field. And we were there for almost three days without food, without water, except for the rain that came, which drenched us.

"After two days, the Gestapo came and made a selection. Part of the people were taken away with the transport, and part of the people were still sent back home to do their work, to do whatever the Germans needed us to do.

"The selection was terrible. There came a group of SS men and few of the big shots, Obersturmfuhrer, and the Jewish Police. They stood and everybody went by. One went this way to the right; one went this way to the left. We didn't know which the right side was to go, which was the good side, and then the

Germans let us go. Men were sent out to go back home too. Certain men were sent home. I guess the Germans took the older people, maybe people that didn't look well or healthy.

"Then there was that time when the big transport came. It was big. I would say half of the city, half of the population of the city, was shipped away. We found out later that all the people went to Auschwitz."

Anja Lewkowics, Blima Fischer's mother

Zindel Lewkowics, Blima Fischer's father

144

Josef Lewkowics, Blima Fischer's brother, in 1938

Melissa Lewkowics, Blima Fischer's sister, in 1938

Blima's interview with the Shoah Foundation continues here:

"I was still with my family, with my father and mother, with my brother and sister. They took my Grandmother Tamara that time, and she was sent away to Auschwitz. Probably, she couldn't walk. We saw her walk when the Germans were taking them to the transport. She was the last one. She could hardly walk, but she walked. She walked. And that was the last time we saw her.

"Afterwards, there were transports going one after another. More and more and more people were rounded up and shipped out. And in the beginning of 1943, they started sending notices home to people. They want this-and-this person to come. Everybody had like a passport, an identification card with a picture.

"We got that notice. The notice said, if you won't come to this-and- this point, they'll come and they will take the whole family. I got the notice to go to the labor camp. The Germans had the list of people who were still around. They ordered all the teenage girls to the local police station. When I got that notice, I went. My mother packed me a small suitcase with some clothes. My entire family walked me to the police station, my mother and father, my brother and sister. We said goodbye and we cried. We were hysterical as we said goodbye because we didn't know if anybody was going to come back. My mother wished me I should have good luck, mazel. That was it.

"A few days after I reported to the police station, I was sent to a transient camp. From there I was picked and away to a labor camp. First at one, and then to a second one. I never saw my parents or any of my family again. I was in the camps for almost two and a half years.

"That day at the police station was the last time I saw any of the members of my family. This was the greatest shock of my life. I never recovered from this trauma. I have carried the horrors and the loss of my family throughout my entire life and will until I pass away. The shock of it all was so great that I can't relax. My insides are always tight. I have had headaches and emotional stress throughout my entire life. There is nothing I can do to change what happened. All I can do is try to be smart. Try to survive. Try to stay alive.

"The Germans had a point where everybody came into the camp system first. It was in a different city, in Sosnowiec. From there, we were sent to a transient camp, where the Germans would come and pick who they wanted for the labor concentration camps.

"There was a men's camp on one side and a women's camp on the other side. They picked out two hundred girls. We didn't know that we were only two hundred. They picked us out like in a selection this one, this one, that one. We were lined up, and he pointed with a finger this one, that one, this one. We were rounded up and sent to a camp where there was a factory that needed labor cheap, or for nothing. We didn't get paid. They told us how to use the machines, the looms, and how to work. The Germans sent us to a factory. They showed us how to work, and that is what we did.

"That first camp was on the Czech border. The name of it was called Gellenau. We were two hundred women, two hundred girls. I don't know if there were married women there, maybe a few, they had to be young. We were all young sixteen, seventeen, eighteen. I was nineteen.

"They gave us something. We never menstruated in the camps. They put something in the food. We knew. That we knew. That we just knew. They put something in the food for us not to menstruate. So we didn't have a problem. But we had problems if we got sick. If we had diarrhea, if we worked on the Appelplatz, the roll call area, and we needed to go to the bathroom, we couldn't go. If we marched to the factory from the camp, if somebody needed to go, there was no way that they would stop or let her go. It was horrible that a thing like that happened. It was horrible because they had to make in their pants. It was horrible.

"We had no privacy. No privacy at all. We had no clothes. We were the same. They left us in our original clothes that we brought from home, but they took away the rest. We had a change of clothes, and we had to wash what we took off and change, and this is how we sustained ourselves for over two years.

"It was a tremendous amount of work, working in the camp. The camp was part of a factory town actually, where they brought the cotton. The cotton was spun to yarn. The yarn was made into fabrics. Then the fabrics were dyed and printed and sent out, wherever. We don't know where.

"But they told us. They had German workers in the factory, and they showed us. We had a learning period for one week. They told us how to lock the threads, how to use the machines, which were giant looms, and then they put us to work. I was working by eight looms. Each loom was like two and a half yards, maybe, long, and we had to watch the spool that was going back and forth on each machine. If a spool broke, we had to stop the machine, rethread it, and let it go again.

"We worked in the factory from six o'clock in the morning until six o'clock in the evening. Twelve hours a day. We were woken up early in the morning. They gave us like fifteen minutes to get washed and to get ourselves together. We used to run to the washroom in the coldest, freezing weather. We had cold water. We had no hot water. And we had to try to keep clean. So we washed. We got dressed. And we had to stand for *appell*, roll call, to be counted. I don't know how long we stayed at the *appell*. Then they gave us a cup of coffee, and we marched to the factory.

"In the factory, at least when it was cold outside, we had warmth. We were working. We didn't know what was outside, what was going on, on the outside, at all. Our life was to get up in the morning, to get dressed, to go to *appell*, to march to the factory, and spend the day in the factory.

"During the lunch hour, we used to get soup in the factory. When we came home, we got a piece of bread in the evening, and that sustained us for two and a half years. Some days we got a baked potato. We got a piece of meat, not all the time, but sometimes. And Sunday was the day when we had to clean our barracks, to clean our quarters. In the first camp, in Gellenau, we were living twenty-four girls in a room, and we had double bunks. There were only we two hundred girls.

"In the second camp, where we were in the concentration camp already, but we were working for the same owners of the same factory, just in a different town. We were thirty-six girls in one room, and we had three bunks in height. And the system was the same as in the first camp. We were woken up early in the morning, we went to the factory, we worked, and we came back. When we came back, we were able to wash up a little bit, and we had a piece of bread that they gave us.

"We used to talk to one another. We used to try not to think about what's going on in the outside world. We had no contact with anybody because there was no mail. There were no letters. There was nothing. It was a prison. We weren't able to get out. We were fenced in, and we had SS women watching us, guarding us. So we weren't able to go anywhere. That's where we stayed.

"The SS women that were guarding us were nasty, mean. If somebody got out of line, she got a good beating. And we were lucky. We were praying not to get sick because if you got sick and you went to the hospital or infirmary, to the *Revier*, the Germans came, picked you up, and they sent you away because you were useless. You couldn't work, you couldn't produce, and so you went. Everybody was trying to keep well as much as they could, and we were young, and we were healthy.

"I had a friend in Gellenau that got sick, and we tried to keep her hidden so they shouldn't know that she was sick. She developed TB and she was going down, down, down. We couldn't hide her anymore.

They took her. They sent her away with the sick transport. She never made it. Quite a few girls got sick. That's why we tried to keep healthy as much as we could.

"There were also Jewish women that were put in charge. There was a Jewish *lager-entess*, a committee, and there were the girls. Each room each *stuba*, the room with the thirty-six girls had a girl, a *stuba-rentesta*, which was like an overseer, over the group that was in that room. We tried to keep out of their reach, and out of their way, as much as we could, because if we got caught by one of them, we were finished.

"In Gellenau and in Langenbielau I was in charge of the loom machines. It was the same factory with the same owners. They had a factory in Gellenau and they had a factory in Langenbielau. And the same two hundred girls that came from Gellenau worked in Langen-bielau because Gellenau was a labor camp. Langenbielau was a labor concentration camp where there were already 1,200 women, not two hundred. And there were different factories that the women were working in, and the same two hundred women worked in Langenbielau in the direct factory like we worked in Gellenau.

"I learned a trade: weaving. I was a very good worker. I was very handy at home with knitting. My mother used to say, 'What the eyes see, the hand can do.' After a while, I was taken away from the machines, and I was doing the repair work. So I was walking around through the factory. If somebody had a break in the fabric, we used to go over, me and another girl, and we would thread it, and put the machine back to work. If something in the machine was broken, we called the *meister* (the foreman or boss), and he came and fixed it.

"From the two hundred girls, not everybody was working in the *va-beri*. Some were working in the *spinnerei*, where they were spinning the yarn, and some were working in the dye factory, where they were dying the fabric, and each group had a different assignment. And we, the Jewish people, kept their factories going. And at the end of 1944 into 1945, when the Russian front was coming closer, they were trying to dismantle the factory. They stopped the factories three months before liberation, and we were all sitting in the camps, not going out, not going anywhere. There was a terrible, terrible demoralization and a terrible time, and we were crying, screaming, 'We are not going to make it. They're going to kill us. They don't even take us to the factories anymore.'

"They picked a group of girls, I think there were thirty of us, and they took us out of the camp, and we were helping with packing and disassembling the machinery. They were trying to ship them deeper into Germany because the Germans didn't think that they were going to lose the war. But then the Russian army came closer and closer and closer, and the war ended.

"We were hungry all the time. Some girls managed when they got their bread, they ate it, the entire portion. They couldn't save it. They ate it up the minute they got it because they were starved. We were starved. Some of them had enough willpower. I was a little girl. I didn't require a lot of food, but I was always hungry. Always. The girls used to go out at night and steal. There was a storage area for potatoes which was covered with earth. So the girls used to go out, and we used to keep watch, and they would steal a pail of potatoes. We had an oven, and we used to put them in the oven to bake them. We used to help ourselves to eat, but this wasn't done very often. This was done only once in a while. And that's how we sustained ourselves. It wasn't easy. It was very, very hard. Very hard. Each day we got a cup of soup, a piece of bread, and a cup of coffee. Sometimes in the kitchen, if we knew somebody in the kitchen, they threw you a piece of bread, or they called and gave you a little soup, but this was rare. It wasn't often that you got that. It was tough. Two and a half years tough. And when we came out of the camps, we were starved, starved, starved. But you can't fill up a stomach all at one time. It took a little time. We made it.

"But the conditions in the factories were good. They were clean. The bedrooms were clean, and they had German people working there. They had Czech people working in the factories together with us too. Well, actually not together, but in the same factory. And sometimes one of those people would bring something from home and throw it to us. A piece of bread, a little soup. Nobody could see it because the machines were tall. They were very big so they couldn't see from the outside what was being done inside the factory. So people tried. Some of the people tried to be nice, but how can they feed two hundred people?

"You couldn't sit down. There was nowhere to sit down. The only break we got was when we went to the bathroom. We would sit a few extra minutes longer than we were supposed to in order to rest up a little bit because we were on our feet twelve hours a day. With the going and coming, it was like fourteen hours. We had no shifts. We had one shift the whole day.

"I was never in a camp where they were burning bodies. I never went to Auschwitz or to any other camp, but you had to know how to direct your life, not to get caught with anything, not to do anything that wasn't right because if you got beaten up, you got sick afterwards.

"We had an experience, my aunt and me. A German woman left us a pair of slippers because the shoes we had were starting to go. They started to rip like a pair of straw slippers. So my aunt picked them out and started wearing them. She put a piece of cotton tied around, and she got caught with that, with those slippers. The Germans wanted to know who gave it to her. Naturally, she wouldn't say, so she got beaten up, and they took her and cut her hair. Being that I was her niece, they figured that we must have something to do with somebody from the workers of the factory, so they cut my hair too. This was the worst experience for me. I cried and cried for weeks, for weeks, until my hair started growing back a little bit. And everybody kept telling me hair grows back, hair grows back.

"Then we found out that a transport of Hungarian women was coming to our camp from Auschwitz. Beautiful, young, good-looking women came. We saw the way their hair was cut and the way they were dressed. It was horrifying. The tall ones wore short dresses with a red painted cross across the front and the back. Naturally, their heads were shaven completely. The short women had long dresses. They carried the shoes on their shoulders because they didn't fit. Those who had big feet got small shoes, and those who had small feet got big shoes. When they came into the camp with us, they started exchanging their clothes, because that's all they came with from Auschwitz, a dress and a pair of shoes.

"This was the first time we first saw what was going on in the outside world. So we saw that we weren't yet that bad off. As bad as it was, we were much better off than the others that were going through the *Fenitos*, or death camps, like Auschwitz or whichever other camp.

"There were things we have to do to make sure that we wouldn't do anything that would get us in trouble. When you saw one of the SS women, you had to stay, to not move. Just stay and wait and see what she would do. You tried to keep out of their reach. You tried to make sure they should not see you. You tried to be invisible. You tried to be on the Appellplatz on time. Whatever you did, you tried to be on time, so you wouldn't get caught doing anything wrong. And as long as you did everything that was expected of you, nobody touched you. You went to work. You made yourself useful for them. You did your job as best that you could, and that's the way we survived. We didn't know that we were going to survive. We didn't know if the Germans were going to kill us in the end. We didn't know that.

"Every night there were people in the factory that would say, 'Just keep it up. Just keep it up. It's not long anymore. The war is coming to an end. It's not long anymore.' They gave us hope that the war wouldn't last very much longer, and that we should keep ourselves strong and try to make it.

"But we were very lucky that the Germans didn't round us up and send us on the march in January when they were sending so many others. That march killed thousands and thousands of people because it was wintertime. They weren't dressed for winter. They didn't have the right clothes. They didn't have any food on the way, and people were just disintegrating, falling like flies.

"When we used to go to the factory in the morning to work, we used to see the transports going by, the groups with the SS. We used to take whatever we had left. We always left a piece of bread from the night before for the morning, so when we got our coffee, we would have that piece of bread with the coffee or we might bring that piece of bread to the factory. Sometimes we would take that piece of bread and try to throw it to other prisoners. If the guards caught one of us bending down to pick up the bread they would shoot us.

"So the pictures weren't very pretty, and we were hoping and praying, praying that the Germans were not going to send us away because we were all in this together. We were 1,200 women, and we were trying to survive. Just trying to survive. And if they would have sent us away, we would have never made it.

"We thought about a lot of things. We thought about home. We thought about where our parents were, where they went, and what is happening. We cried our eyes out plenty, and we didn't know what the next day was going to bring or what they were going to do with us. We were never sure that we were going to live to the next day. We were never sure. But somehow, somehow, we made it. In spite of what they wanted and in spite of what they did, we survived.

"We didn't hear much from the women from Auschwitz because they weren't there long enough. They were Hungarian women. Germany occupied Hungary in 1944. They were rounded up and sent to Auschwitz, and they worked there for a day or two. They were lucky to get out. Not all of them got out. Some of them got out, and the rest of them went to the gas chambers. They were lucky to get out. Even though they weren't there very long, just by looking at them, we learned enough.

"They didn't speak our language. They spoke Hungarian. We didn't understand what they were saying. We spoke Yiddish and Polish. If there had been one maybe that spoke Yiddish, we could converse a little bit. But they didn't see much of Auschwitz because they were rounded up, I guess, and brought to Auschwitz. And in Auschwitz they only spent a day or two, just long enough for them to take away their belongings, to shave their head, to give them their clothes, and to send them out with the transport. Five hundred women came to us from Auschwitz.

"We first really found out what had been going on when we came out, after we were liberated. We knew that if you went to Auschwitz, you didn't come out. But we didn't know exactly what they were doing, how they were killing. We didn't know. I don't think we knew. I remember that we tried not to get caught, to not get sent out, but what they were doing, that there were gas chambers, I don't think we knew that. I don't remember knowing exactly what was being done in Auschwitz. We first found out after we were liberated, after we started meeting people from different areas and from different camps. There were hundreds of camps. It wasn't a single camp. There were hundreds of them.

"I just met a girl that was from my town that went away from Benjin two weeks after me. She was sent to a camp, a small camp. Then she was transferred and was sent on the march. She wound up in Mauthausen, in Austria. So I was very fortunate. I really was very fortunate that I stayed in that one particular camp, first in Gellenau and then in Langenbielau, and that is where I was when we were liberated by the Russian army.

"After Langenbielau, what happened next is a long story. We were liberated by the Russians. There were four, maybe six officers that came into the camp. They didn't know where they were going. They were looking and going, and they found a camp.

"We were all assembled. We already knew that the war was coming to an end. We already knew because the SS disappeared two days before and they emptied the food magazine. We knew we were on our own. The *stub-rentesta* kept saying, 'Please keep calm. Don't start running out. You don't know what kind of army, what kind of soldiers, or how long they have been on the fronts. You don't know how hungry they are for women. So please stay put. Stay together.' But we were hungry and needed to eat. We went out through the wires. We cut the first three and pulled a few apples, we pulled the fruit. We pulled whatever we could and brought it into the camp.

"Never, never will I forget that moment when these few Russians came into the camp, and we were only women. There were no men. We were flung in the air [by the soldiers] like bulls from happiness, from joy that we finally came out of the prison, that we would most likely be free people. And slowly, from the different camps, people started coming and looking. Who is in this camp? Who is in that camp? We thought that we could find family. This was the hardest time for me. I found out that nobody from my family survived and that I was the sole survivor. This was the hardest. I didn't know where to go. I didn't know what to do. I was free, but I had nothing. I had nobody. A friend of mine survived with her mother. The mother took me in, and she said, 'You can stay with us as long as you have to, as long as you need.'

"But I had no peace. I knew that my mother did not survive because I had records that she was still in the ghetto at the end of 1943. I knew that the ghetto was liquidated and everyone was sent to Auschwitz. So I knew that my mother and all the children did not survive, but I was hoping that my father would be somewhere. So I started to search.

"I went back to Benjin, right after the liberation, maybe a week after liberation. Many others went back with me. We had no tickets on the train. We had no money to buy tickets. We used to get on the train, and as the train was going, we went with it. The trains didn't go through because the train lines were broken up during the war. So the train would go for like an hour, an hour, and a half, maybe two hours. Then it stopped and we had to go to a different point, wait three or four hours and then continue. It took two weeks for me to get back to Benjin.

"When I came into Benjin, the city was like a ghost town. There was nobody there. There were no people. I looked into the courtyards through the gates and they were empty. Nobody was there.

"I found out that there was a Jewish committee. So I walked from the tram line, not even the train station, and the trolley took me to Sosnowiec, into Benjin. I walked because I wanted to see whether I would see somebody in the street. I went to the Jewish committee and there I saw somebody that knew my father. He said to me, 'Your father is alive. You'll find him. Your father is alive.' I left my name on the list that I survived and if somebody was looking for me, that I was there. I didn't know where I was because I had no address. I had no place to live, and I could not go to the house where I had lived. I turned back, hysterical, crying. I never went back to Benjin again. I went back to Langenbielau. I stayed with my friend and her mother, and I was looking for a way out of there. I didn't want to live there. I didn't want to stay there. I wanted to get in into Germany. And I was still hoping that somewhere, someplace, I'd find my father. My father must have been, at that time in 1945, forty, maybe thirty-nine years old. So I figured that I would stay for a little while. Then somebody told me that they'll take me across the border to Germany.

"I went with a group of people. There were nine of us. We went through Czechoslovakia. We were stopped on the Czech border and searched. My friend had some money, and they took it away from him. Then we stayed in Prague in a Red Cross hotel for a few days. It was like a transient camp. People were coming through from all over.

"A boy came through. I remember I had washed my blouse, the one that I still had from the concentration camp. I had washed it and asked if I could use an iron. I was ironing and a boy came in and he started talking to me. He asked me where I was from, what I was doing, and where I want to go. He said he would take me across the border. The group, everybody that I was with, kept saying, 'Go ahead. Go. You don't have to wait here. We don't know when they are going to take us out of here.' So I went, and he brought me into Austria, to Linz. He said that from Linz there were transports every few days that were going into Germany. He said to me, 'I have some friends here in the city.' I put down my belongings, whatever I had in a backpack, and he said to me, 'I'll take you to the camp. I know some girls there. So you'll be able to lodge with them together.'

"I left my things in Linz, and I went with him to the camp. He introduced me to the girls. There were four girls in a room in that camp. They were like stables, like horse stables really, that they had put up as barracks. I don't even remember their names anymore. I stayed with them a few days, maybe more than a few days, because we were fighting to get quarters, better quarters for the survivors than the stables that we were in.

"They didn't build a camp in Linz, but it was small houses they gave us, and they made something like a Displaced Persons Camp for us. But when I came to the girls, I slept through the night, and the next day I went back to Linz because I wanted my things.

"I met Mayer. Mayer was living at the camp. He was one of the friends, and after that, it is history. I went back to the camp and later we were relocated to Bendinmichel. We got decent quarters. I was assigned to a house. I got a room and privileges for the kitchen. Mayer and I courted for eight months. After that, after I met him, I didn't miss anything anymore. I had enough food and I had enough to eat. I missed my family. They didn't make it. They didn't survive. Mayer and I started to build a new life.

"We got married in June 1946. Bendinmichel was built right after President Truman became president and we lived in Bendinmichel until September 1947. In 1947 I became pregnant. I was five months pregnant when we decided to leave Linz and go into Germany. We had friends working for Haganah, and there was a transport going to America. In Mannheim there was a transient camp where all the people went through, and they said, 'We'll take you to Germany. We'll take you to Munich.' I had two cousins in Frankfurt and Saltzheim.

"My Aunt Sarah, my mother's youngest sister, survived together with me in the camp and a cousin of mine. My mother's sister's daughter was also in the same camp. They live in Israel. My aunt's name was Sarah. Rosenberg was her married name. She died in 1993. My cousin's name is Rose Muir. They live in Netanya in Israel, and they also built a family. They left Germany and went to Israel. This was the extent of the family that I had left.

"From Munich we went to Frankfurt, and we got a room in Saltzheim, in the camp. We stayed there as long as the camp was in existence. When the camps were dismissed and diminished, we went into the city, into Frankfurt, and stayed there until 1949. In October 1949 we sailed for America. Mayer's sister had already been in America for two years and she sent us an affidavit and went on the Displaced Persons on Truman's quota to the United States. Truman was able to bypass restrictive immigration quotas and allowed 100,000 displaced persons to be admitted to the United States not coming from any country. Therefore there was no quota restriction. Truman was clever! My daughter was born in Germany, at the beginning of 1948, and was already twenty months old when we came to America.

"We came to the States in 1949. We established a life here. We were two families, my husband, and his brother. My brother-in-law had a small grocery store, and we took over the store. Mayer went to work immediately the day after we came in. We came in on a Saturday. Sunday morning he went into the store.

"But when we got off the ship my daughter had a high temperature. She got sick, and I needed a doctor, and I needed a bed. I didn't have a crib for her because my brother-in-law and sister-in-law lived in a furnished room, and they got us a room in the same house. The room was like a two-by-four. There was no crib. My husband and my brother- in-law went and bought a crib, and they carried it on their backs, back to the house so that I could have it for the baby.

"My sister-in-law called a doctor. He came and he examined my daughter. She had come down with measles after the trip from Europe. We lived in that furnished room for two months. Then we got an apartment. Barry was born in 1951 in September. I was busy raising two children.

"I didn't tell my story for years. I just couldn't bring myself together to talk about it. Mayer used to tell the children his experiences of the camps and what he went through. I never did. But not long ago, when it all came out in the open, when the organizations started forming, The Warsaw Ghetto Assistance, the organization in New York. That's when it came out, I would say, about fifteen years ago, in 1980, but not before. I never talked about my past and never talked about my experiences during the war to my children.

"The first few years after liberation not only did, I not talk about it, but my nerves were shattered. Shattered. I was suffering so, and I was taking medication, antidepressant. I was a young person, and I kept it buttoned up in me. I couldn't get myself to bring it out.

"I told my story twice, maybe not to such a degree and in such detail as now, but I told my story twice to the doctors for restitution. Not to such an extent and not in such a broad scope as this, but I was asked many questions about my experiences and what I went through. And just recently I talked to a doctor about all this. And because he kept asking questions and he kept prying and prying and wanted to know more and more, I told him. But afterwards I was sick. I was just sick.

"The entire two and a half years of the occupation were a miracle. It was a miracle that anybody survived. I remember the roundups when the truck used to come. We used to run and hide so we wouldn't get caught in the street, because once you got caught you were put on that black wagon, you were finished. This I remember.

"My only hope in telling my story is that there is never going to be anything like what happened during World War II to the Jewish population. There's nothing that I could say to them. I'm just praying that it should never happen again because there's nothing much to say.

"What else can you say?" Anna.

At the hospital in Frankfurt, Blima could look out and see the Mein River. The trees that grew along the river were large and the red-roofed buildings that lined it complemented the natural features of the land.

In the small hospital room, there was an unspoken tension in the air. The war was still in the back of every German's mind, and Jewish people were a reminder of things that many wanted to forget. The doctors, nurses, and other patients all had an apologetic manner. But Blima and I had no hard feelings towards them.

I, Mayer, waited in another part of the hospital because they did not allow husbands in the birthing rooms at that time. I watched people come and go as I waited. Since meeting Blima, I had done all that I could to make her life comfortable. Now we were creating a family. I couldn't help but think about life as I sat and waited. All the lives that were gone, and now a new life. I looked at my hands and then rubbed my head and felt the bump there, a lifelong reminder of the ill-natured Ukranian SS man who had slammed me with his rifle butt because I had chosen too small a stone that fateful day at the Mauthausen quarry.

When Blima's time came, she birthed the baby without difficulty. A nurse came to me and told me that I could see her. Blima and the baby were in the bed, surrounded by blankets. She smiled at me and then down at the baby.

"It's a girl, Mayer," my wife said, her face radiant. "It's Anna."

Anna Fischer, 1949

Anna Fischer, 1949

Anna Fischer, 1949

Anna and Mayer Fischer, 1949

Anna and Mayer Fischer, 1949

Blima and Anna Fischer, 1949

Mayer Fischer, 1949

Anna and Blima Fischer, 1949

Oskar Schindler

After the war, Oskar Schindler came to our house and requested that Nathan and I sign a petition to save his life. He wouldn't look us in the eye. My brother and I refused to sign for him. But my best friend, Al Bukiet, and 950 other Jews that were saved by Schindler, all signed and asserted that he was a righteous person. He was liberated in Czechoslovakia. My memories of Oscar Schindler are that he was an opportunist. That when the Nazis were in power, he aligned with them. He acted as one of them. When the Nazis were losing control, he helped the Jews.

Israel

"You had the feeling there, that you were home."

When Blima and I were in the DP camp, there came a time when we had to choose where we wanted to go to make our permanent new home. We had opportunities in America and Israel. I had planned on going to Israel. Israel was not a state yet, and I wanted to go and be involved in the war there. I even had two guns that I planned to take to Israel, before they were confiscated in Germany.

After I got married, however, I changed my mind and decided on America. President Truman had signed a bill allowing 100,000 displaced persons to come to America, and Nathan, Lydia, and their spouses were going there.

Over the following years, Blima and I had the opportunity to visit Israel ten times. We felt at home there, as Jews and as people. In reality, it was a second home. Every Jew in the world could go to Israel and have dual citizenship. This was a promising idea for me: that I could always go home to a state that was our Jewish state.

Blima Fischer's visit to Israel, 1965

NINE

WORK AND LIFE IN AMERICA

Blima cooked every day always something fresh and good. We had no problems. We had a house with Italian marble in the front of the house. When I bought the house, I paid cash.

After the war, several hundred thousand Jews lived in DP camps, and much of the world tried to help, but not everyone.

Great Britain kept their doors closed, as they did during the war, admitting only a small quota of Jewish immigrants each year. Many Jews went to Israel. Some started life over again in foreign lands as far away as China. But Blima, Anna, and I headed to America. We brought whatever we wanted and whatever we could. When we reached America, we found Americans welcoming and ready to give us even more.

As the ship pulled into New York harbor I realized that there were flags waving and an orchestra was playing, for us. It was a giant celebration to greet the last boat carrying the 100,000th immigrant. There were WWII veterans and other young soldiers lined up as we disembarked. American flags hung from every rafter, blowing in the sea breeze. I felt a surge of excitement, after many locked down days at sea. As I exited the ship with Blima and Anna, a man with a camera jumped in front of us.

"Can I take a picture of your little girl for the paper, sir?" he inquired.

We smiled proudly, holding little Anna in a white dress knitted by Blima.

"For the newspaper?" I asked.

"Yeah, look at her, look at all of you. Perfect picture! Welcome to America."

There were so many people, and so much excitement. A man from a Jewish organization approached us next and said, "This way. There is a bus that will take you to a hotel. This is where you want to go."

But we were looking for Lydia.

Blima and I were both shorter than most of the crowd, but at last we saw her.

US naval ship, USS General R.L. Howze. Mayer, Blima, and Anna were brought to New York from Frankfurt on this ship courtesy of Harry Truman. October 1949.

NATION WELCOMES ITS 100,000TH D. P.

He Is an Estonian Farmer Who Arrives on Army Transport With 1,352 Refugees

The 100,000th displaced person to be admitted to the United States was among the 1,352 refugees who arrived yesterday morning aboard the Army Transport General Howze, which docked at Pier 60 at West Twentieth Street.

Theodore Klisk, 50 years old, an Estonian farmer, head of a family of four, had the distinction of being the 100,000th refugee admitted under the Displaced Persons Act of 1948. His arrival was marked with special ceremonies aboard the ship and on the pier.

Greetings to him and the other refugees were extended by Harry N. Rosenfield, a member of the Displaced Persons Commission; Raymond M. Hilliard, Commissioner of the city's Department of Welfare, and representatives of various agencies assisting the immigrants on their arrival in the United States. The Fire Department band played while the ship was being docked and in the intervals between speeches.

Another refugee who came in for special attention was Israel Weisler, 70, of Niska, Austria, who was greeted by his brother Samuel Weisler, 68, of 218 New Lots Avenue, Brooklyn. The brothers had not seen each other for fifty-one years. The immigration of Israel Weisler was arranged by the Hebrew Immigrant Aid Society, 425 Lafayette Street.

The Howze passenger list included 145 children under 6 years old and 120 between 6 and 15. Nationalities represented were: Polish, 391; Ukrainian, 261; Latvian, 215; Lithuanian, 175; Estonian, 80; Russian, 63; Hungarian, 25; Czech, 23; German, 23; Yugoslav, 16; Roumanian, 9. There were also forty-one stateless persons on the ship.

The occupational skills of the wage-earners among the new arrivals included: skilled workers, 208; personal services, 159; agricultural, 114; unskilled laborers, 118; clerical, 37, and professional, 26. The immigrants will make their homes in various states.

Theodore Klisk, an Estonian farmer who was chosen for the honor, is welcomed by Estonian Relief Minister, Edward Magi, as he comes down the gangplank of the steamer General Howze with his wife and three sons.

The New York Times

The New York Times
Published: October 30, 1949
Copyright © The New York Times

New York Times *article confirming the arrival of Army Transport USS* General R. L. Howze *at Pier 60 at West Twentieth Street. October 30, 1949.*

After the war, my sister Lydia remarried a man named David Wolf, a Hungarian Jew. They came to America before any of the Fischers. David had bought a grocery store in a very poor, quite dangerous neighborhood, and when Nathan and I came over, we bought it from him. Nathan and I worked six days a week. The grocery store was located on Marcy Avenue and Green Avenue in Brooklyn, New York. One of our customers was the heavyweight boxing champion, Sonny Liston.

We worked very hard to support our families. Blima and I had Anna, and then Barry. Nathan and his wife, Luba, had Rose and Harry to take care of. We knew how to work hard, and we worked the grocery store for a while. We were happy to have a way to support our families. One day in 1950, a male customer came into the store and picked up a few cans of tuna fish. He put three cans on the counter and two cans in his pocket. Nathan asked him if he was going to pay for the two cans of tuna fish in his pocket. He wasn't going to let him get away with it. The customer responded by pulling out a knife. Nathan picked up a metal cage used at the time to carry milk bottles back, which was recycled with the milk deliveries, and he put it between himself and the customer for protection from the knife. They stood there looking at each other, this milk bottle cage between them. My brave brother wasn't going to have made it all this way to be killed by a customer in a grocery store. Nathan called out, "Mayer! There is a crazy out here with a knife." He said all this in Yiddish so the customer couldn't understand him.

I came out quietly, picked up a quart bottle of beer, and smashed it on the customer's head, knocking him unconscious. Bleeding, he fell to the ground. Nathan and I carried him out to the curb and locked the door. I looked at my brother and said, "It's time to sell the grocery." It took a few months, but it was sold. Now we needed to decide what we would do next.

I was friendly with a man who owned a company called Rogers Tobacco, Candy, and Stationery Inc., which delivered candy and cigarettes to our grocery store. After a few meetings, Nathan and I used the cash we had from the grocery store proceeds and invested in a three-way partnership with Rogers Tobacco's owner. Two years later we bought out our partner and continued to operate the business for thirty-five more years, still under the name Rogers Tobacco, Candy, and Stationery. We worked hard, six days a week.

I had a police permit to carry a pistol because I carried a large sum of money in cash and checks to the bank, three times a day. We had a warehouse full of cigarettes and at the time a whole carton, wholesale, was about $3.00. Cigarettes were gold at the time and we had 6,000 square feet of products from drug sundries to school supplies, and we had a lot of people coming in to buy over the counter and wholesale.

We had several robberies and attempted robberies. During one of the robberies at Rogers Tobacco, around 1970, thugs came in with guns. They were holding up Nathan, who was always in the front, while I was in the back, counting money. I heard some kind of ruckus and I looked outside. I saw that there was a guy with a gun. I whipped out my gun and shot at the guy. One of the robbers shouted, "Hey! There is a guy in there shooting at me!" And they all ran away.

My sister Lydia was married to David Wolf, and they were well-known entrepreneurs. They built the famous Wolf's Delicatessen chain in New York City. He built them, built up the volume, and then sold them. David and Lydia had one son, Marvin, who became a hippie a classical Eastern Indian musician who studied under the virtuoso Indian musician/instructor Ali Akbar Khan, learning to play the sitar, and is now a dive master on the Island of Grenada, completely loving life. David died from heart disease in 2000 and my beloved sister Lydia died in 2007 from complications due to Alzheimer's disease at the age of ninety-five.

Mayer and Anna Fischer with Roger's Tobacco truck, 1957

Rose, Harry, Luba, and Nathan Fischer. Harry Fischer's bar mitzvah, 1968

Extended Fischer Family, including nine concentration camp survivors, 1968.

Barry

Barry was born on September 7, 1951. We named him *Baruch*, after my father. Baruch in Hebrew means "blessing." Almost every prayer in Hebrew begins with the word Baruch.

Barry was born in Ocean Hill-Brownsville in the Women's Hospital located on Eastern Parkway. We lived at 507 Bristol Street, Brooklyn, New York. We rented a second floor apartment in a brick brownstone. The landlords were Fannie Kaplan and her husband a wonderful couple. They were close friends and part of the family Fannie taking the role of confidant and babysitter.

When Barry got older, I took him on delivery routes with me and eventually gave him his own route. He was the first one in our family born in America, and I knew Barry's experience growing up was very different from mine. But I never wanted him to forget his heritage.

When he was four years old, I began to teach him about my life story. Barry would sit on my knee in our living room, and I would tell him all the events that happened: my life in Krakow, the ghetto, my smuggling, how I survived. I told him about how my father Baruch died, how I met his mother, and all about daily life in the concentration camps, including the torture, the search for food, and how I survived emphasizing that every day was my last day, so I took risks every day. I watched my son's face, amazed, shocked, and sad. I shared my pain with each story. I shared, knowing Barry would retell this story, praying that the world would never forget what happened, so it would never happen again. That was my prayer! That was my hope! By sharing my experiences, I would protect Jews forever. Never again!

Barry Fisher, newborn, 1951

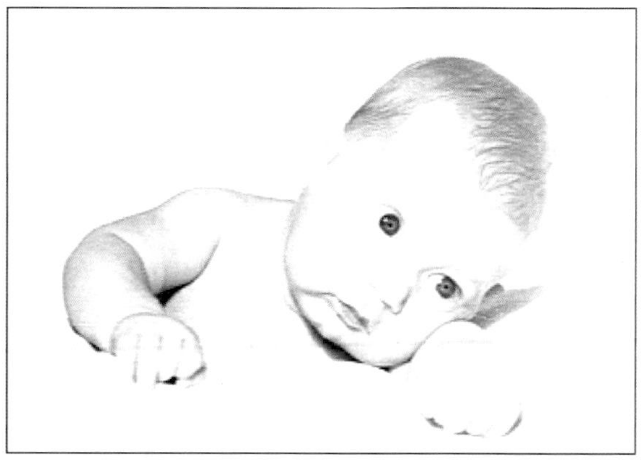

Barry Fischer, newborn, 1951

*Anna and Barry
Fischer, 1954*

Barry Fischer, 1954

Through the Eyes of My Son – Life in America

I grew up working in my father's business. Rogers Tobacco operated as a wholesale distributorship of cigarettes, candy, tobacco, stationery, paper goods, cigars, and so forth. They sold goods to grocery stores, candy stores, restaurants, and stands in many buildings in Manhattan. I remember the smell of the warehouse, in the humidor room. We had a room that was filled with cigars of all sizes and shapes from the Caribbean and Central America. An endlessly running humidor intensified the warehouse's sweet, pungent aroma of cigars.

As a boy, I wanted to be with my father. He worked six days a week. I missed him, so to see him more often, I asked if I could work with him on Saturdays. And I did, consistently, from the age of five until I graduated from Brooklyn College.

My father and uncle were busy. They had ten employees, three trucks, and a station wagon. The warehouse was like a fortress with alarms and steel gates. The alarm would often go off in the middle of the night, and my father and I would rush to the warehouse to make sure every- thing was okay. The alarm was loud and the brick warehouse was cold, especially in the middle of the night. The police usually were there to meet him. My father was very friendly with all of the local policemen. They would come in and buy boxes of cigars and candy, which we sold to them at cost, or sometimes gave them as gifts. Of course, when they came in the middle of the night, my father would give them a gift.

I loved working with my father. We received boxes of Chiclets, Hershey bars, Chuckles, Pinwheels, baseball cards, every brand of candy, cigarettes, tobacco, and cigars imaginable, as well as pens and school stationery, and paper goods. We had it all! I would cut open the boxes and pack out the candy in boxes on shelves for customers to buy or for workers to assemble packages on the counters.

I was good at my job. I learned to tie filled boxes, and to cut the rope using my hand without using a knife. The trick was to hold the rope, crisscrossed on itself around my hand and palm, and pull, and the rope would cut itself.

My father was the outside salesman at Rogers, and my Uncle Nathan was the inside man. They never took extended vacations until I turned seventeen and could drive. I would cover for my father on the outside, and my father could substitute for my uncle on the inside. I was very proud that they trusted me with so much responsibility at such a young age. I became the person to visit the customers and carry money to the bank three times a day. I was seventeen years old and trusted to carry $100,000. I learned to be aware, to look around, to make sure the coast was clear to be sure, to park close, and to never show what I was carrying in a plain brown bag.

My father had an amazing sense of direction, and he knew the streets of New York City well, especially Brooklyn, Manhattan, and Queens. I was the only one that could ever understand the manner in which he gave directions. "On your way to Queens, just on the way to deliver to one of our customers, make a right, turn at the light," I can still hear him saying in his rapid-fire way. "Go straight until you see the Esso gas station (usually he gave me the wrong name of the station), make a right, go four blocks, and then make a left and it is right there. You can't miss it." Uncanny as it was, 99 percent of the time I understood and found my way. At the beginning, he also came with me on routes and showed me short cuts.

A few times after I started to drive, he came with me on a route, and he was still able to show me better short cuts, so I could get from one store to the other more quickly. From when I was sixteen years old, my father sent me to represent him and Rogers to any government authority that needed to get information from him regarding such things as defending him against parking tickets, the tax authority, and licensing when he needed me to put a tax stamp on the bottom of cigarettes he sold. My father trusted me, that I could do a good job.

My father collected cash and checks, as much as $100,000 a day. He would go to the bank three times a day to deposit the money, and he was always concerned about being held up. His partner and brother Nathan were often armed robbery targets, both in and out of the store, so my father carried a gun. Once, a gunned man came in, and my father shot at the fleeing bandit.

Over time, my father came to believe that "The Nazi's didn't get me, but they will kill me if I continue with Rogers Tobacco." One night while I was in law school in Los Angeles, I dreamt that my father was injured. When I called to tell him about the dream, and to see if he was okay, he said, "I am not surprised. You're my son, and we are connected." He had been seriously hurt, and almost killed.

Mayer Fischer after being attacked and robbed. Brooklyn, New York, 1982

One Monday in 1985, my father went to his brother's house to pick up money from collections on Saturday. Two armed men followed my father and attacked him. He was badly beaten after they wrestled his gun away. They took approximately $50,000 in checks and cash.

After that incident, my father understandably did not want to work anymore at Rogers Tobacco, a small company that my father and Uncle Nathan had built into a business that brought in gross sales of $12 million a year. After running the business for thirty-five years, my father at the age of sixty-five and my uncle, age sixty, both retired. They sold the business assets to a competitor.

My mother and father were very good at buying and selling homes. When they came to the U.S. in 1949, they rented a small apartment on the second floor of a brick walk up in Brownsville. I was born at the Women's Hospital located on Eastern Parkway, just down the street from the Lubavitch rabbi and his temple and 100,000 followers. Our landlady, Fannie Kaplan, became my godmother and often babysat for me.

My mother would take me shopping on Pitkin Avenue. I remember my mother was a perfect dresser: designer clothes, always perfectly matched colors, shoes, pocketbook, belt, and clothing. She always did the same for me, taking me to the finest stores on Pitkin Avenue to buy Italian shoes and imported clothing.

My father would take me to Livonia Avenue to buy fresh bread, and to a special pickle store that had barrels and barrels of pickles. Sour pickles, the best pickles in the world! The men that owned the pickle stove looked like rabbis with long black beards. They always gave me a free pickle. My father would also take me under the old, elevated train on Livonia Avenue, near Fortunoff's, to the small department store that had everything from crystal to cooking utensils and everything else under the sun.

In 1955, my parents moved from the apartment on Bristol Street and bought a duplex house in the Flatbush section of East 57th Street, Brooklyn. We lived there for sixteen years.

I had about twenty-five friends my age living on our E 57th Street block. We walked to school together and played football, basketball, and baseball. I had a great childhood.

The 1960s brought the war in Vietnam. My father told me that no matter what, he would never let me go to war. "I lived through a war, and you never will," he said defiantly. I was lucky because the army developed a "bingo" lottery draft. My birthday was number 251, and they only drafted people up to around 120. I was never called off to war. In later years, I would hope that my son, Bennett Joseph Fischer, would never be called off to war, even though he is registered for the draft.

I was swept away in the counterculture of the 1960s, and my parents faced another challenge: how to deal with me! Until I was seventeen, I followed my parents' plan. But at eighteen, I branched out, becoming not quite a hippie, but I sure did love the good ol' Grateful Dead!

Brooklyn College was easy for me, because I expected to take over my father's business, so I just didn't think I needed to work hard. It wasn't until my senior year, after my father started thinking about selling Rogers Tobacco that I started to think about career options. For several years I dabbled in import/export ventures, and then, in 1986, I became an attorney, specializing in family and civil law.

My parents sold their Flatbush duplex and bought a beautiful single-family house on "the (Long) Island" in North Woodmere, also known as "the Five Towns." It was very upscale. My father loved to sit in the garden and enjoy the flowers, like the purple, blue, and white bougainvillea's. I could see he was proud of and very peaceful in his own garden. They later sold the North Woodmere house and purchased a small home in Cranbury, New Jersey, to be near my sister.

Then came another Jewish migration, especially of Holocaust survivors, from New York to Florida. They then sold the Cranbury house and bought a condominium in Hallandale, Florida. My parents were both active. There are many organizations in Miami, including The Krakow Society. They had many friends, most of them also survivors, living very active lives in Florida. Survivors trusted other survivors. They understood each other. They had gone through the Holocaust, the Nazi terror, and all had a new life in America.

TEN

LIFE CHANGED

One morning following a large snowfall from the night before, I opened the door to the quiet, snow-lit neighborhood. There was a thickness to the air and to each step I tried to make as I walked to the car. The snow was wet, heavy, and thick, and still falling. It was so quiet out that I could hear the snowflakes fall on my eyelashes and on the arms of my coat.

I had never missed a day of work. I had had only one hospital stay in my life, and that was when I couldn't pass a kidney stone and they had to remove it. I was scheduled to open the warehouse and Nathan couldn't do anything until I got there. I went to the garage for a shovel, following my own footsteps and using my arms to balance as I lifted my knees high, careful to retrace my movements. I carried the shovel back to the truck and leaned it up against it. I opened the door, figuring I might as well warm the vehicle up first, but when I put the key in the ignition nothing happened. I tried again. The engine turned over and over until, at last, it caught.

I got out and cleared off the truck. The snow landed in heavy heaps as I cleared the windshield, windows, and hood. I shoveled as quickly as I could to dig it out. It was such wet snow. I dug and dug around the tires, pile after pile. The neighborhood was no longer silent, but all I could hear was my loud breath and my heart beating. I knew Blima was inside, worried. I could feel her worry.

There! I thought triumphantly, seeing the job was done. *I can go.*

I stood upright, stepped into the truck, and blacked out.

The cold and stress had caused a minor stroke. After that, I stopped making jokes and smiling all the time. It was a bad incident, but it was also a catalyst for change. I wanted to stop working in Rogers Tobacco. God had given me a sign that the time had come to do so.

Blima

"Everything I did was for her."

Blima was an amazing chef, and she was always singing while she whipped up delectable dishes. I didn't think my voice was as good as hers, so I would just listen. She did the singing in the house, just like my mother. We listened to classical music and went to concerts, like we had when we were courting. I believe that music extended our lives.

Blima was expert with her hands. She was good at any kind of handiwork. She always made beautiful things for our children and grandchildren. This was true even before the war, and during the war it saved her when the Germans put her to work in a factory. Blima didn't talk about the war to our children, though. She left that to me. I was the one who would make sure they never forgot.

My secret to staying happily married for sixty-four years was simple: Avoid disagreements. We would argue and bicker almost daily, but at the end of each argument we agreed on what was important to us: being together. You have to always give in. Life is for a family filled with love, not for arguments. Besides, I found that Blima was always right anyway. I attribute it to her being a mother with special intuition. She would have feelings about things, and things always came out right.

Life After Retirement

After I retired, I couldn't stand the idea of sitting at home and not working. I was still in good health and felt much too young to "cash in my chips." So I did what anyone else who was young at heart would do: I bought an ice cream shop in Greenwich Village! I thought ice cream seemed like a friendly business to try. Everyone liked it. So we sold gelato (Italian-style ice cream) at a shop that was near a movie theater. Every day there were lines of people out the door to buy gelato, even in the winter. They were wearing scarves and wool coats, but they still wanted gelato.

We had a few employees, but Blima and I were there all the time. Chocolate, macadamia nut, vanilla, strawberry, whatever people liked, we had it. Everyone left smiling.

One day Barry came in looking for me. He found his mother serving customers in the front.

"He's in the back," she said, dishing up a scoop of chocolate on top of a scoop of mint with a waffle cone on top, while a small Irish woman watched, critically but pleased, with a look of total anticipation.

Barry stepped around the counter and into the back room. There he found me lying on the floor, sleeping in front of the freezer. He said I was on my back, eyes closed … and sound asleep! The ice cream business apparently was almost too much for me. Barry was worried but tried to joke about it. Working for the Nazis didn't kill me, but the ice cream business had me lying on my back by the deep freeze. I sold the shop shortly after that. I had hoped it would keep me busy, but after a year, I realized that I didn't need to be so busy, and maybe it was a little too much.

In 1970, when I was still running Rogers Tobacco, Nathan, and I, and two other survivors, started a business building homes on Long Island. I was always interested in being a builder. My whole life I wanted to do it. I had worked as a carpenter before and during the war. Once retired, I finally felt free to do it. We built three homes in Merrick that sold quickly, and profitably. The four partners were Nathan and I, Joe Schweitzer the plumber, and Manny the butcher.

After that, we reinvested our profits and built twenty-five homes. Sadly, those homes did not make much profit. But at least I did get to see what building was all about.

Finally, I quit working. We were living in New Jersey then, and I realized that my wife was sitting home alone during our retirement. She wanted to spend more time with me and kept talking about moving to Florida. So we did.

Once in Florida, my only job was to shop with Blima. Shopping, shopping, and more shopping! Blima was the boss. We also played a great deal of cards, like poker. We went to different hotels with friends and played. We even went on gambling cruises. Sometimes we would take a plane to the Bahamas at seven o'clock in the evening and spend all night in the casinos, and in the morning the plane would take us home. I never had a gambling problem. For Blima and me, the social aspect of playing games of chance was the most fun—though winning ninety-nine percent of the time I played didn't hurt either.

Blima and I knew many people in Florida, most of them were other survivors. We preferred to be around other survivors. We didn't trust anyone else, perhaps because we knew that no one else could really understand what we have been through. It was also our way of taking care of each other. We made sure to keep our money in the family, or among other Jews.

2009

Losing Blima in 2009 was a shock to me. I never expected her to go first. All my life, I prepared so Blima would have everything she wanted after I died. When Blima first got sick, the doctors were not able to find what was wrong. There were a series of x-rays, other tests, and then she was diagnosed with pancreatic cancer. The doctor told us she only had a few months to live. They put her on a schedule for chemotherapy for three months. We expected three months of life, but she got twelve nearing the end. Blima wouldn't have anything more to do with the hospital. I had nurses and everything brought into our house, twenty-four hours a day. She told her nurses stories about her life. She used to crack them up and make them cry. She told them about the time I first saw her with her little bag, and how I said I was going to take care of her.

"And he always did," said Blima. "He always did."

When she died, I gave the nurses some of Blima's designer purses. Blima passed away on Saturday, November 6, 2008, in our own home. It was so hard to say goodbye, to let her go, but I had no choice. God took her. It was her time.

The first few days were hard. You expect your friends, your family, the Jews to mourn with you, after all we have been through together— Krakow, the camps. The Krakow Society, a group of survivors, was having a party the same day as Blima's funeral. I would be mourning the death of my wife, honoring her life, and they would be having a party. They should be at the funeral, and I should be with my friends at the party on another day. We had always been together this way. We started the Krakow Society in 1963 in NYC to commemorate the survivors of Krakow. I was one of the guys that started it. We supported them all the time, and this once I asked a favor—for them to come to my wife's funeral—and they didn't change the date of the party.

I talked to my friend Ralph about it several times. I just lost my wife. I wanted to see my friends. Krakow is important to me. But they said they wouldn't cancel the party.

It's hard not to hold a grudge about such things, when people are supposed to pull together. Still, there were many friends at Blima's funeral. I will never forget the image of wheeling Blima's coffin from the chapel to the gravesite, with my father walking beside the coffin as it rested upon a stainless-steel movable table with crisscrossed accordion supports.

ELEVEN

MY ADVICE ON HOW TO LIVE, I MADE IT TO 94!

"Every effort in life makes a difference."

I still go to Friday night services and shul every Saturday, out of respect for my parents and the religion they taught me. I lost faith in God during the war, but as they say, "you never know." So I go.

I like to think I am well-known and well-liked. People know I am a good man. Some say I have a cute smile and a subtle sense of humor. At the retirement home, people talk about me, they all know who I am, and they all respect me. They all ask for a copy of this book. On my ninetieth birthday, everyone cheered, "Happy birthday, Mayer!"

Women talk as they play cards. Word gets around. Everyone is looking for a boyfriend. But I am not interested. I don't even look.

I play cards with a group of other old men, veterans of various wars. Most of them are wisecrackers at this age, but it is clear that they love each other. I never miss a card game. For my friends, I am always there to help. A perfect example is when an old friend asked me to keep him company on a drive to the airport, just in case he couldn't make it. He was terrified to go alone, so I went with him. I am the kind of person people want to come along. One other time, a neighbor couldn't walk, so I brought her food, until she could do it herself. This is life at ninety-two. It ain't bad!

Legacy

"The best thing about being ninety-four is that every year I am alive, I am still defeating Hitler."

Hitler killed twenty people from my immediate family in Krakow, about three-fourths of my family. From my wife Blima's family an additional twelve immediate relatives including her sister Melissa, her brother Joseph, her father, Zindel, and her mother, Anja/Anna were lost. Now, I am the proud father of two (Anna and Barry), grandfather of five (Melissa, Ian, Sean, Bennett, and Bella), and great-grandfather of nine, and with more to possibly come.

When asked what kind of legacy I want to leave my family, I say I've had a good life, despite what I went through in the war, and I hope they will remember, and will still be Jewish.

I still want to live. Even at ninety-four years of age I pray for five more years.

To those who may read this after I am gone, I give this advice: You must always be strong in your mind and about what you want to accomplish. You never have to give in. Try to do it the way you expect it. Every effort in life makes a difference.

I wouldn't be alive today, except God blessed me. I thought I was going to die in the concentration camps. Every day was hell. But every day, I took a risk, knowing that taking risks in life can make the difference between life and death! I chose life! And so did God!

I once said that if I made it through the war, it would be important to tell my story. People need to know what happened. The normal human mind cannot picture or imagine what happened in the concentration camps. What happened in the

Holocaust is not what normal people think up. When I say that now, it is not because I want the last story, but that these things actually happened. People need to know what happened. People need to realize that it can happen again.

I made it through the war and I told this story to my children and grandchildren, but I also tried to tell them much more through my actions. From the example of my life, I hope you learn what else is possible, such as sixty-four years of marriage, an honest life of work, good credit and good business, the respect of friends and associates, and life. Even just living is the difference.

Mayer Fischer family at the Flagler Hotel, South Fallsburgh, New

Anna Fischer at the Flagler Hotel, South Fallsburgh, New York.

Melissa Metrose on her wedding day

Anna Fischer-Metrose's three children, Ian, Melissa, and Sean Metrose, on Melissa's wedding day

Mayer and Blima Fischer, 2000

Ian Metrose, Mayer Fischer, Michael Metrose, Sean Metrose, Bennett Fischer, and Barry Fischer

Bennett Fischer, 1996

Mayer, Blima, and Bennett Fischer lighting candles. Bennett Fischer's bar mitzvah, 2005

Barry and Bennett Fischer lighting a candle. Bennett Fischer's bar mitzvah, 2005

Mayer and Blima Fischer, Bennett Fischer's bar mitzvah, 2005

Bennett and Barry Fischer with sister Anna's family, (from left to right: Madison Fink, Michael Metrose, Ian Metrose, Laure Metrose, Mayer Fischer, Blima Fischer, Bennett Fischer, Melissa Fink, Jarad Fink, Christina Metrose, Sean Metrose, Anna Metrose, Barry Fischer)

Extended family, Bennett Fischer's bar mitzvah, 2005. (from left to right: Michael Metrose, Mayer Fischer, Ian Metrose, Blima Fischer, Bennett Fischer, Melissa Fink, Sean Metrose, Anna Metrose, Barry Fischer)

Barry, Mayer, and Bennett Fischer, 2011

Mayer Fischer's ninety-second birthday, 2011

Mayer Fischer's ninety-second birthday, 2011

Barry and Bennett Fischer, 1996

Mayer Fischer's ninety-second birthday, 2011, (from left to right: Michael Metrose, Melissa Fink, Madison Fink, Christina Metrose, Ian Metrose, Sean Metrose, Anna Metrose, Mayer Fischer)

Barry and Bennett Fischer, 2011

Mayer Fischer with Michael, Sean, and Ian Metrose, Mayer Fischer's ninety-second birthday, 2011

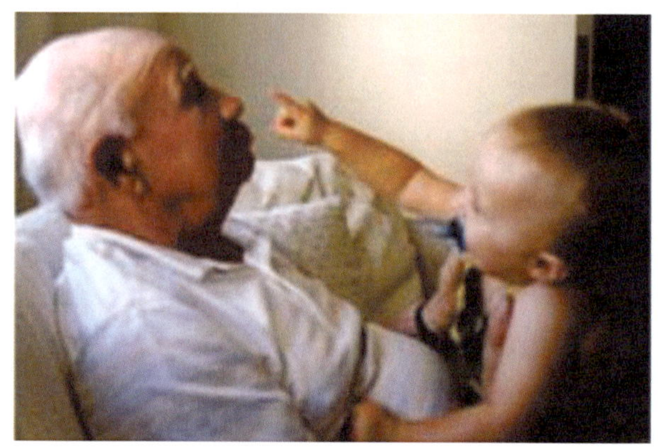

Mayer and Bennett Fischer, 1993

Bennett, Barry, and Mayer Fischer, Mayer Fischer's ninety-second birthday, 2011

Bennett Fischer and Bella Fischer, 2013

Mayer and Bennett Fischer, Mayer Fischer's ninety-second birthday, 2011

*Mayer Fischer and his great granddaughter, Madison Fink, Anna's granddaughter,
Mayer Fischer's ninety-second birthday, 2011*

Anna Fischer-Metrose's son, Sean Metrose, and family, 2011

Barry and Mayer Fischer

Blima and Mayer Fischer, 1989

Mayer, Blima, Anna (holding Madison Fink), and Barry Fischer, Bennett's Bar Mitzvah, 2005

Mayer and Barry Fischer, 2005

Barry and Mayer Fischer

Mayer Fischer

TWELVE

BARRY'S VISIT
TO THE CAMPS

Barry went to visit the concentration camps at Mauthausen, Melk, and Ebensee in 2004.

The man behind the desk at the hotel in Vienna, Austria, listened politely and attentively to Barry's story about my father and me.

"I want to visit all of these concentration camps—Melk, Mauthausen, and Ebensee."

"Yes, Herr Fischer," the clerk replied. "The camp in Melk is closed but let us see what we can do to help you."

Barry smiled. "That would be nice. Most particularly, I want to see Melk."

From the time Barry knew why he was given his name, until this moment, he felt a need to see the place where Baruch had died. He was driven by this primal instinct in the same way that birds migrate, or how monarch butterflies follow the migration of their dead ancestors. In the same way that salmon return to their birthplace, humans seem driven to find their own history.

The hotel clerk knew the woman who took care of the grounds at Melk. Though the camp was closed to visitors, Barry was able to visit by paying her for her time to open it for him.

The town of Melk was quaint. There was openness to the countryside and quietness to the atmosphere. The town of Melk overlooked the army base which once had been the Melk Concentration Camp. Strange really, considering the atrocities and deaths that occurred there. There was only one building left, the crematorium.

Barry was shown to the crematorium. It was small. Much smaller than he had expected. He asked the woman if he could be alone there for a while. The oven was small and slightly narrow, no bigger than a kitchen table. The walls were covered with photographs hung survivors, placed in tribute by the loved ones of people who had died there. Barry took his time and looked at the photographs. He turned back and looked at the oven. It was so small. He couldn't get over how small it was.

All the people that they killed there, and it's so small.

This is the place where I had received a pot of soup, in exchange for wheeling in the body of my dead father, delivering him to the crematorium.

Every detail of my stories came into perfect clarity for Barry. My father's injury while he was working as a slave. How the *blockmeister* sent him to the infirmary. The medic giving him an injection of gasoline, not medicine. His murder. Carrying him to the crematorium and getting a pot of soup as a reward. Celebrating my father being released from this hell.

Through the war and devastation, the German records somehow survived. Their impeccable record-keeping showed the organization behind their efforts. The records of every imprisoned Jew—how many hours each worked, and when and where they died—had somehow survived.

After the Warsaw Pact, the German government began making reparation payments. To this day I still receive a pension for all of the work I did in the concentration camps. I am being paid for having been a slave.

I remember my number: 84674.

If you go to the U.S. Holocaust Museum in Washington, DC, type in my number: 84674.

I leave you with this. I beat Hitler by staying alive!

I have my family. Hitler did not take my family away from me. Hitler tried to rob me of everything, but he couldn't. Thank you, God!!